LEARN SPANISH

Nicole Irving

Designed by Russell Punter
Illustrated by Ann Johns

Language consultants: Esther Lecumberri
& Jacqueline Devis

Series editor : Corinne Stockley
Editorial assistance: Lynn Bresler
Pronunciation advice: Jane Straker

Contents

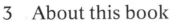

3   About this book

4   Spanish pronunciation guide

5   Understanding grammar words

6   Nouns

8   Adjectives and first verbs

10   More about verbs

12   Whose is it?

14   Telling people what to do

16   Asking questions

18   Negatives

20   Stem-changing verbs

22   Prepositions

24   Reflexive verbs, "who" and "which"

26   Saying what you are doing

28   Personal pronouns

30   Past tenses and adverbs

32   The imperfect tense

34   The preterite

36   Irregular preterites

38   The perfect tense

40   The future tense

42   More about the future

44   Making comparisons

46   The conditional

48   A letter to read

49   Spanish grammar summary

56   Answers to quizzes and puzzles

58   Numbers and other useful words

59   Spanish–English word list

About this book

This book will teach you all the important first steps in the Spanish language and give you plenty of opportunities to try out what you are learning.

Pages 4 and 5 contain a Spanish pronunciation guide and an introduction to grammar. Try out the sounds introduced in the pronunciation guide before you start the main part of the book.

The section on grammar explains basic grammar words. It will help you if you do not know anything about grammar or if you want to remind yourself of what words like "noun" and "subject" mean.

Page 6 is where the main section starts. Each double page explains certain points about Spanish, so your knowledge will build up as you go through the book.

On each double page, the characters in the picture strips say things that show how the language works in practice. The Speech bubble key gives you translations of what they are saying, but you should try to understand them first, and only use the key for checking. Any new Spanish words that crop up are shown in a list with their English translations, and there is always at least one test-yourself quiz to help you try out what you have learned. (The answers are given on pages 56–57.)

In the Speech bubble key, you will sometimes notice a slightly different translation from the word-for-word one. This is because different languages do not always say things in the same way, and the translation given is more natural in English.

The characters

In this book, you will meet various characters. You can see the main ones on this page.

The first two you will meet are Fede and Carmen, as they fly to Villatorres from Madrid. They are on their way to the Salchicha house where they are going to spend a few days. Follow their story as you progress through the book.

Fede Molinero
Carmen's brother. Likes walking, climbing, cycling and eating.

Carmen Molinero
Fede's sister. One year older than him. Likes reading crime novels.

María Salchicha
Fede and Carmen's friend. Met them last year in Madrid.

Alicia Salchicha
María's mother. Quite a well-known sculptress. Runs the house on a shoe-string budget.

Pedro Salchicha
María's father. Son of Santiago Salchicha. Works for a charity.

Ramón Robón
An international crook. On file at Madrid headquarters.

Guau Guau
The Salchicha dog. Tireless and brave, if a bit excitable at times.

Kiti
The Salchicha cat. Inquisitive, likes being pampered. Loves teasing Guau Guau.

Key

This book uses a few shortened words and symbols that you need to know about:

m stands for masculine, **f** stands for feminine, **sing** stands for singular and **pl** stands for plural;
* after a verb means it is irregular in the present tense. (Words like "masculine" and "irregular" will be explained when you need them.)

Spanish pronunciation guide

Pronunciation is how words sound. In Spanish, many letters are not said in the same way as in English.

The list below shows you how letters are said. Letters missing from the list sound the same or nearly the same as in English. Bear in mind, though, that people may also say things differently depending on where they come from.

Learn these tips little by little and try out the words given as examples. If you can get a Spanish speaker to help you, ask them to make the sounds and say the words so that you can copy what you hear.

Vowel sounds

In Spanish, vowel sounds are always short:

a sounds like "a" in "cat", for example when used in *la* and *una*;

e sounds like "e" in "let", for example in *el*, *le* and *torre*;

i sounds like "i" in "machine", but shorter, for example in *camino*;

o sounds like "o" in "hot", for example in *alto*;

u sounds like "oo" in "root", for example in *un* and *una*;

Groups of vowels

When in Spanish you have two or more vowels together, you usually pronounce each vowel in turn. For example, **eu** is said "e/oo" as in *Europa*, and **iu** is said "ee/oo", as in *ciudad*. The same applies to double vowels, for example **ee** is said "e/e", as in *leer*.

Consonants

c is said as in "cat", for example in *casa*. However, before "i" or "e", it sounds like the "th" in "thing", for example in *cinco* and *cesta*;

ch sounds like the "ch" in "cheese", for example in *chico*;

g is like in "good", for example in *gato*. However, before "e" or "i", it sounds like the "ch" in the Scottish word "loch", or a bit like the "h" in "hate", for example in *general* and *girar*. When "g" is followed by "ue" or "ui", the "u" is not sounded but it makes the "g" sound like in "good", for example in *guerra* and *guitarra*;

h is not sounded at all, for example in *hola*;

j is said like "ch" in the Scottish word "loch", or a bit like the "h" in "hate", for example in *jardín*. It is the same sound as a **g** before "e" or "i" (see **g** above);

ll sounds like the "y" in "yes", but with a hint of an "l" sound in front (a bit like the "llia" in "brilliant"), for example in *ella*;

ñ is like the "ni(o)" sound in "onion", for example *mañana*. The sign that goes over the "n" to make it sound like this is called a tilde;

qu sounds like the "c" in "cat", for example in *pequeño*. It is the same sound as the **c** in *casa* (see **c** below left);

r is an "r" sound made by putting your tongue on the ridge just behind your top teeth, for example in *barca*. When **r** is at the start of a word or when you have **rr** in a word, the "r" sound is virtually trilled (your tongue is in the same position, but you make it vibrate), for example in *ropa* and *perro*;

s sounds like the "s" in "same", for example in *cansado*. However, before "b", "d", "g", "l", "m" and "n", it sounds like the "s" in "trousers", for example in *desde* and *mismo*;

v sounds like the "b" in "bad", for example in *viejo*;

y sounds like the "y" in "yes", for example in *yo*. However, when it is used on its own, as a word (to mean "and"), it is said like the Spanish **i** (it sounds like the "i" in "machine");

z sounds like the "th" in "thing", for example in *zapatillas*. It is the same sound as a **c** before "e" or "i" (see **c** above left).

Getting the stress right

When speaking Spanish, it is very important to stress the right part of each word. Normally, for words that end in a consonant other than "n" or "s", you stress the last syllable (part of the word) for example "*mir*" in *dormir*. For words that end in a vowel or "n" or "s", you stress the second-to-last syllable.

Any Spanish word that does not follow this pattern is written with a stress mark (´), or accent. This shows you which part of the word you should stress, for example in *árbol*. A stress mark is always placed over a vowel.

A few words have a stress mark that is over the part of the word you would stress anyway, for example *éste*. These stress marks are used to make a clear written difference between two words that sound the same and would otherwise look the same, but have different meanings. For example, *este* means "this" and *éste* means "this one".

Grammar is the set of rules that summarize how a language works. It is easier to learn how Spanish works if you know a few grammar words.

All the words we use when we speak or write can be split up into different types.

A **noun** is a word for a thing, an animal or a person, for example "box", "idea", "invention", "cat" "woman". A noun is **singular** when you are talking about just one, for example "box", "cat", "woman". It is **plural** when you are talking about more than one, for example "boxes", "cats", "women".

A **pronoun** is a word that stands in for a noun, for example, "he", "you", "me", "yours". If you say "The dog stole your hamburger" and then, "He stole yours", you can see how "he" stands in for "dog" and "yours" stands in for "hamburger".

An **adjective** is a word that describes something, usually a noun, for example "pink", as in "a pink shirt".

A **verb** is an action word, for example "make", "run", "think", "eat". Verbs can change depending on who is doing the action, for example "I make", but "he makes", and they have different **tenses** according to when the action takes place, for example "I make" but "I made". The **infinitive** form of the verb is its basic form, for example "to make", "to run" or "to eat". Dictionaries and word lists normally list verbs in their infinitive form.

An **adverb** is a word that gives extra information about an action. Many adverbs describe how a verb's action is done, for example "slowly", as in "She opens the box slowly". Other adverbs say when an action happens, for example "yesterday", or where, for example "here".

Prepositions are link words like "to", "at", "for" and "near".

Subject or object?

When used in a sentence, a noun or pronoun can have different parts to play. It is the **subject** when it is doing the action, for example "the dog" in "The dog barks" or "he" in "He barks". It is the **direct object** when the action is done to it, for example "the dog" in "He brushes the dog" or "it" in "He brushes it".

There is also an **indirect object**. In "He gives the dog a bone", "the dog" is an indirect object ("a bone" is the direct object). You can normally tell an indirect object because it could have a preposition, such as "to", "at" or "from", in front of it, so in the example above, you could say "He gives a bone to the dog". A pronoun can also be an indirect object, for example "him" in "Give him the bone", which can also be said "Give the bone to him".

Nouns

In Spanish, all nouns are either masculine or feminine. This is called their gender. The words for "the" and "a" show the gender.

"The" is *el* with masculine nouns and *la* with feminine nouns.

"A" (or "an") is *un* with masculine nouns and *una* with feminine nouns.

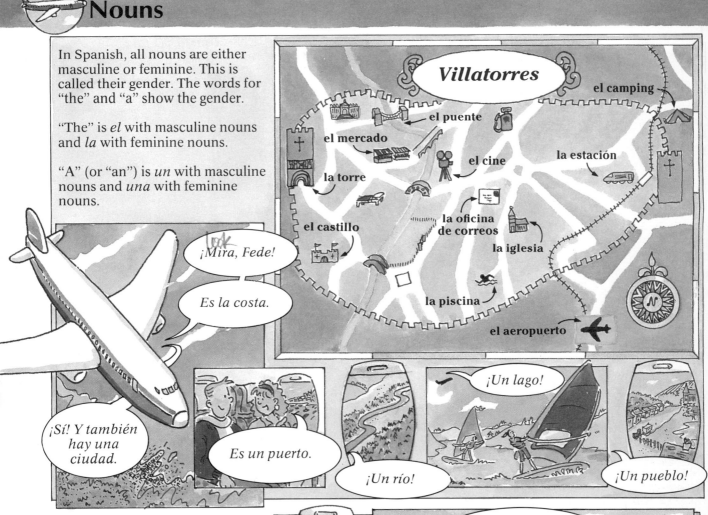

Plural nouns

In the plural, most Spanish nouns that end in a vowel add an "s" on the end, and those that end in a consonant add "es".[1]

In Spanish, the word for "the" changes in the plural. It is *los* with masculine plural nouns and *las* with feminine plural nouns.

"Some" is *unos* with masculine plural nouns and *unas* with feminine plural nouns.

Spanish question marks and exclamation marks

In written Spanish, you do not just put a question mark (?) or an exclamation mark (!) at the end of a question or exclamation. You also put an upside-down one (¿ ¡) at the start.

1 For more about plural nouns, see page 49.

Learning tip

Try and learn nouns with *el* or *la* in front of them so you know the gender. Many words change to match the noun's gender, so getting this right will help to get other words right. For many nouns, you can guess the gender by looking at the ending. Most nouns ending in "o" are masculine and most nouns ending in "a" are feminine.[2]

New words

el mercado	market
la torre	tower
el castillo	castle
el puente	bridge
el cine	cinema
la oficina de correos	post office
la piscina	swimming pool
la iglesia	church
la estación	station
el camping	campsite
el aeropuerto	airport
la costa	coast
la ciudad	town
el puerto	port
el río	river
el lago	lake
el pueblo	village
la montaña	mountain
el caramelo	sweet, candy
el mapa	map
la casa	house, home
el hotel	hotel
el café	café, coffee
la granja	farm
la carretera	road
el camino	path, way
el campo	field, countryside
el bosque	forest
la isla	island

mira	look
es	(it) is[3]
son	(they) are[3]
sí	yes
y	and
también	too, also, as well
hay	there is/are
ahí	there
están	(they) are[3]
dos	two
está	(it) is[3]
¡qué bien!	great!
¿qué es eso?	what is that?
aquí	here

Getting to the Salchicha house

For some strange reason, the man in the seat behind Fede and Carmen is looking at their map and memorizing the route to the Salchicha house. He has found the first of the six landmarks that show the way from the airport. Can you find the other five? List them in Spanish, making sure you use the right word for "a".

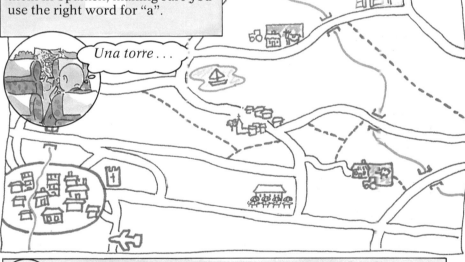

Speech bubble key

- *¡Mira, Fede!* Fede, look!
- *Es la costa.* It's the coast.
- *¡Sí! Y también hay una ciudad.* Yes! And there's a town too.
- *Es un puerto.* It's a port.
- *¡Un río!* A river!
- *¡Un lago!* A lake!
- *¡Un pueblo!* A village!
- *¡Oh, montañas!* Oh, mountains!
- *¡Mira! Es Villatorres.* Look! That's Villatorres.
- *Sí, ahí están los puentes . . .* Yes, there are the bridges . . .
- *y las dos torres.* and the two towers.
- *¡Oh, ahí está el aeropuerto!* Oh, there's the airport!
- *¡Qué bien! ¡Caramelos!* Great! Sweets!
- *¿Qué es eso, Carmen?* What's that, Carmen?
- *Es el mapa.* It's the map.
- *Y aquí está la casa Salchicha.* And here's the Salchicha house.

2 *El mapa* (map) is an exception. For more tips to help you work out the gender of a noun, see page 49. 3 *Es* and *son* mean "(it) is" and "(they) are", and so do *está* and *están*. This is because Spanish has two verbs for "to be", *ser* and *estar* (you will find out about this on page 8). With *aquí* (here) and *ahí* (there), you use *está* and *están* (from *estar*).

Adjectives and first verbs

In Spanish, adjectives usually follow the noun.[1] They also agree with it. This means the adjective (normally) matches the noun's gender and is plural if the noun is. Most adjectives have a masculine form ending in "o" and a feminine one ending in "a" (the rest stay the same in the two genders). In the plural, adjectives ending in a vowel add "s" and those that end in a consonant add "es".

Ser and *estar* (to be)

Spanish has two verbs "to be". *Ser* is used to say what a person or thing is and where they are from, and to describe them. *Estar* is used for things that change (I'm tired, The door's open) and for saying where people and things are.

Las vacaciones perfectas

Un cielo azul

Un mar tranquilo

Una playa blanca

VILLATORRES

Excursiones apasionantes

Ser/estar (to be)

yo soy/estoy[2]	I am
tú eres/estás	you are
é/ella/Ud. es/está	he/she is, you are
nosotros(as) somos/ estamos	we are
vosotros(as) sois/estáis	you are
ellos(as)Uds. son/están	they/ you are

"You", "we" and "they"

Spanish has four words for "you". You say *tú* to a friend and *vosotros* to friends. *Usted* (*Ud.*)[3] is polite and used for an older person or someone you don't know. *Ustedes* (*Uds.*)[3] is the plural polite form. *Nosotros* (we), *vosotros* (you) and *ellos* (they) are masculine forms. For females, use *nosotras*, *vosotras* and *ellas*.[4]

Tener (to have)

yo tengo	I have (got)
tú tienes	you have (got)
él/ella/Ud. tiene	he/she has (got), you have got
nosotros(as) tenemos	we have (got)
vosotros(as) tenéis	you have (got)
ellos(as)/Uds. tienen	they/you have (got)

Tengo un bolso negro pequeño.

¡Eh Fede!, también tienes una tienda.

¡Ah sí! Tengo una tienda verde.

¡Oh perdón!

¡Hola! ¿María? Soy Carmen.

Uf . . . Estoy cansada.

Una maleta verde, un bolso azul . . .

Yo tengo un bolso verde.

Estamos en Villatorres.

¡Qué alto!

Gracias, es muy amable.

---

1 A few Spanish adjectives can sometimes be used in front of the noun (for more about this, see page 49). **2** In Spanish you often use verbs without the word for "I", "you", "he", etc. (you say *soy* and *estoy* instead of *yo soy* and *yo estoy*, *tengo* instead of *yo tengo*, *tienes* instead of *tú tienes*, etc). For more about this, see page 10. To say "it" + a verb (e.g. "It's on the table"),

My, your, his, her . . .

These words are a special kind of adjective. The word that is used depends on the gender of the noun:

(sing m/f)	(pl m/f)	
mi	*mis*	my
tu	*tus*	your
su	*sus*	his/her/its your (polite)
nuestro(a)	*nuestros(as)*	our
vuestro(a)	*vuestros(as)*	your
su	*sus*	their/your (polite)

Mi mochila es roja.

Éste es tu bolso.

No, es su bolso.

Aquí está su maleta, señorita.

Mis maletas son grises.

No, está bien, tenemos tu mapa.

What is their luggage like?

Try to find these people in the picture strips and figure out what their luggage is like (what kind of bag they have and what colour it is). The first solution is *Su bolso es verde*.

New words

las vacaciones	holidays, vacations
el cielo	sky
el mar	sea
la playa	beach
la excursión	outing, trip
el bolso	bag
la tienda (de campaña)	tent
la maleta	suitcase
la mochila	backpack
el maletín	briefcase
perfecto(a)	perfect
azul	blue
tranquilo(a)	quiet, peaceful, calm
blanco(a)	white
apasionante	exciting
negro(a)	black
pequeño(a)	small, little
verde	green
perdón	sorry, excuse me
¡qué!	how!, what!
muy	very, really, most
alto(a)	tall, high
cansado(a)	tired
hola	hello
en	in, at
gracias	thank you, thanks
amable	kind, nice
no	no
está bien	(it's) all right
rojo(a)	red
gris	grey
éste	this (one)
señorita	Miss
amarillo(a)	yellow
marrón	brown

🗨 Speech bubble key

- *Tengo un bolso negro pequeño.* I've got a small black bag.
- *¡Eh Fede!, también tienes una tienda.* Hey Fede! You've got a tent as well.
- *¡Ah sí! Tengo una tienda verde.* Oh yes, I've got a green tent.
- *¡Oh perdón!* Oh sorry!
- *¡Qué alto!* How tall (he is)!
- *Uf . . . Estoy cansada.* Ah . . . I'm tired.
- *Una maleta verde, un bolso azul . . .* A green suitcase, a blue bag . . .
- *Yo tengo un bolso verde.* I've got a green bag.
- *¡Hola! ¿María? Soy Carmen.* Hello, María? It's Carmen.
- *Estamos en Villatorres.* We're in Villatorres.
- *Gracias, es muy amable.* Thank you. You are so kind.
- *No, está bien, tenemos tu mapa.* No, it's all right, we've got your map.
- *Mi mochila es roja.* My backpack is red.
- *Éste es tu bolso.* This is your bag.
- *No, es su bolso.* No it's not. It's his bag.
- *Mis maletas son grises.* My suitcases are grey.
- *Aquí está su maleta, señorita* Here's your suitcase, Miss.

Spanish always uses the verb on its own in the "he/she" form, e.g. for "it is", you say *es* or *está*. **3** The short forms *Ud.* and *Uds.* are often used in writing, but never spoken. **4** For a mixture of males and females, use the masculine forms.

More about verbs

Some Spanish verbs, such as *ser* and *estar*,[1] are irregular (they don't follow a pattern) and must be learned one by one. Most, though, follow one of three patterns according to whether they end in "ar", "er" or "ir". The "ar" pattern is shown here by *andar*. To make the present tense, you add a set of endings to the verb's stem.[2]

Andar (to walk)

yo ando	I walk (am walking)[3]
tú andas	you walk
él/ella/Ud. anda	he/she walks, you walk
nosotros(as) andamos	we walk
vosotros(as) andáis	you walk
ellos(as)/Uds. andan	they/you walk

Andas muy lento.

No, miro el paisaje.

Ah sí, el sol brilla . . .

. . . y los pájaros cantan.

Perdón, buscamos el camping.

Eso es fácil, es todo recto.

Querer (to want)

This is a special verb called a stem-changing verb (see page 20):

yo quiero	I want
tú quieres	you want
él/ella/Ud. quiere	he/she wants, you want
nosotros(as) queremos	we want
vosotros(as) queréis	you want
ellos(as)/Uds. quieren	they/you want

Being polite

To ask for something politely, you use *querer* in a special tense, and say *quisiera* (I would like). See page 46.

"I want to . . ."

To say what you want or would like to do, you can use *querer* or *quisiera* with a second verb in the infinitive, or basic form, for example *Quiero pagar* (I want to pay).

Quiero una mesa a la sombra.

Yo quiero un zumo de naranja muy frío.

More about "I", "you", etc.

In Spanish you often use a verb alone, without the word for "I", "you", "he", etc. On the whole, you only use *yo*, *tú*, *él*, etc, when neither the verb ending nor the general situation tell you who the verb refers to.[4] For "it" + a verb, you always use the "he/she" form of the verb on its own.

Él quiere un té.

Yo quisiera un zumo de naranja.

Nosotros queremos un helado y un zumo de manzana.

Y yo quisiera una coca-cola, por favor.

Quisiera pagar, por favor.

¿Dónde está mi cámara de fotos?

¿Qué queréis hacer ahora?

Yo quiero visitar el castillo.

¡Oh!

Yo quiero ver las tiendas.

1 See page 8. **2** The stem is the infinitive form (the basic form) minus its "ar", "er" or "ir" ending, so the stem of *andar* is *and-*. The pattern for "er" verbs is shown on page 12 and the "ir" pattern on page 16. **3** English has two present tenses. You can either say "I walk" or "I'm walking". Spanish has a similar, second present tense (see page 26), but you normally just use the

Queremos alquilar unas bicicletas.

The mysterious letter

Carmen saw the man drop a letter. This is it. It was written by someone who was really tired and it has lots of mistakes (eight in all). Can you rewrite it correctly and work out its meaning in English?

Una isla desierta, 1893

Mi querido hijo Santiago:

Soy un hombre viejo. Estoy sola en mi isla desierta y mis casa cerca de Villatorres está vacío. Tengo una secreto. Soy muy ricos. Ahora mi tesoro es tu tesoro. Mi casa ocultan la primera pista. En primer lugar tú busco los dos barco.

Adiós

Sancho Salchicha

New words

el paisaje	landscape
el sol	sun
el pájaro	bird
la mesa	table
el zumo de naranja	orange juice
el té	(cup of) tea
el helado	ice cream
el zumo de manzana	apple juice
la coca-cola	coca-cola, cola
la cámara de fotos	camera
la tienda	shop
la bicicleta	bicycle
el hijo	son
el hombre	man
el secreto	secret
el tesoro	treasure
la pista	clue
el barco	ship, boat
mirar	to look (at)
brillar	to shine
cantar	to sing
buscar	to look for
pagar	to pay
hacer*	to do, to make
visitar	to visit
ver*	to see
alquilar	to hire, to rent
ocultar	to hide
lento	slowy
eso	that (one)
fácil	easy
todo recto	straight ahead
a la sombra	in the shade
frío(a)	cold
por favor	please
¿dónde?	where?
¿qué?	what?
ahora	now
desierto(a)	deserted, desert
querido(a)	dear
viejo(a)	old
solo(a)	alone
cerca de	near
vacío(a)	empty
rico(a)	rich
primero(a)[5]	first
en primer lugar	first of all
adiós	goodbye, farewell

Speech bubble key

- *Andas muy lento.* You're walking very slowly.
- *No, miro el paisaje.* No I'm not, I'm looking at the landscape.
- *Ah sí, el sol brilla . . .* Oh yes, the sun's shining . . .
- *. . . y los pájaros cantan. . . .* and the birds are singing.
- *Perdón, buscamos el camping.* Excuse me, we're looking for the campsite
- *Eso es fácil, es todo recto.* That's easy, it's straight ahead.
- *Quiero una mesa a la sombra.* I want a table in the shade.
- *Yo quiero un zumo de naranja muy frío.* I want a really cold orange juice.
- *Él quiere un té.* He wants a cup of tea.
- *Nosotros queremos un helado y un zumo de manzana.* We want an ice cream and an apple juice.
- *Yo quisiera un zumo de naranja.* I'd like an orange juice.
- *Y yo quisiera una coca-cola, por favor.* And I'd like a coca-cola, please.
- *Quisiera pagar, por favor.* I would like to pay, please.
- *¿Dónde está mi cámara de fotos?* Where's my camera?
- *¿Qué queréis hacer ahora?* What do you want to do now?
- *Yo quiero visitar el castillo.* I want to visit the castle.
- *Yo quiero ver las tiendas.* I want to look at the shops.
- *Queremos alquilar unas bicicletas.* We want to hire some bicycles.

*Remember, an asterisk (*) means the verb is irregular.

standard present tense shown here unless you need to stress that the action is actually happening now. **4** You also use *yo*, *tú*, *él*, etc. to draw attention to whoever the verb refers to. **5** When the masculine form, *primero*, is used before a noun, you drop the "o" and say *primer*.

Whose is it?

In Spanish, to say things such as "Fede's sweater" or "Fede's tent", you use *de* (of), so you say *el jersey de Fede*, *la tienda de Fede*. In answer to "Whose is it?", you say *Es de Fede* (It's Fede's) or simply *De Fede* (Fede's).

Using *de* with nouns

You also use *de* with nouns such as "girl" or "boy" to say things like "the girl's sweater" – *el jersey de la chica* (word for word, "the sweater of the girl"). However, *de* and *el*, the masculine singular word for "the", combine and become *del*, for example *el jersey del chico* (the boy's sweater). This means the four different forms for "of the" are *del*, *de la*, *de los* and *de las*.

"Er" verbs

On page 10, you learned the present tense of *andar* (to walk), which shows the pattern followed by regular "ar" verbs (those with an infinitive ending in "ar"). The verb *comer* (to eat – see below) shows you the regular "er" pattern. To make the present tense, you add a set of endings to the verb's stem (the infinitive minus "er").

Comer (to eat)

yo como	I eat (am eating)
tú comes	you eat
él/ella/Ud. come	he/she eats, you eat
nosotros(as) comemos	we eat
vosotros(as) coméis	you eat
ellos(as)/Uds. comen	they/you eat

> *Buenos días. Somos los amigos de María.*

> *Buenos días. Yo soy su madre.*

> *Me llamo Alicia . . . y aquí está nuestro perro Guau Guau.*

> *¿De quién es el gato?*

> *Es de María. Se llama Kiti.*

> *Aquí está la habitación de mis padres, . . .*

> *mi habitación y . . .*

> *la habitación del huésped.*

> *Aquí está el estudio de mi madre.*

> *Aquí escondemos todos los tesoros de la familia.*

> *Y aquí está un retrato antiguo del abuelo de María, Santiago.*

> *Aquí está un cuadro muy viejo de la casa Salchicha.*

> *¡Oh no! Es Comelotodo, la cabra de los vecinos. Come cualquier cosa.*

> *¿De quién es esa ropa?*

> *Es de mi hermano . . .*

This, these, that, those

The Spanish words for "this, these" and "that, those" change according to the gender of the noun you use them with. "This" is *este* [m] or *esta* [f], "these" is *estos* [m pl] or *estas* [f pl]. "That" is *ese* [m] or *esa* [f], and "those" is *esos* [m pl] or *esas* [f pl].[1]

1 Spanish also has a set of words for "that/those over there": *aquel* [m], *aquella* [f], *aquellos* [m pl] and *aquellas* [f pl].

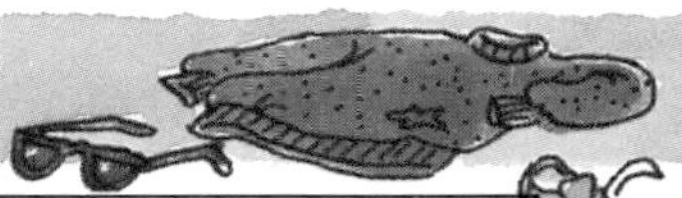

Speech bubbles (picture strip):

y este jersey . . .

¿De quién son estas gafas?

Me gusta esta camisa.

Es del constructor.

Son de Carmen.

Es de Fede.

Me gustan mucho estos catalejos.

Son de Fede también.

La ropa

la ropa	clothes, clothing
el pantalón	trousers
los vaqueros	jeans
la falda	skirt
el chandal	track suit
los pantalones cortos	shorts
el jersey	sweater
la camisa	shirt
la camiseta	T-shirt
la chaqueta	jacket
el traje	suit
los zapatos	shoes
las zapatillas (de deporte)	trainers
el sombrero	hat

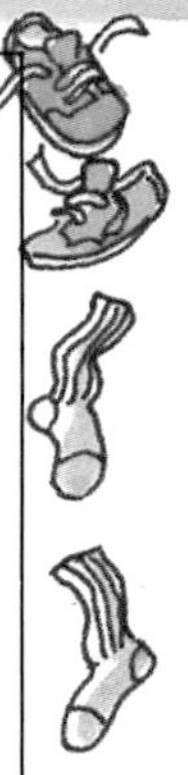

Saying what you like

For "I like" Spanish uses the verb *gustar* (to please), and you say *me gusta* (word for word, "it pleases me"):

me gusta	I like
te gusta	you like
le gusta	he/she likes, you like
nos gusta	we like
os gusta	you like
les gusta	they/you like

If what you like is plural, you add an "n" and say *gustan*.

New words

la chica	girl
el chico	boy
el amigo, la amiga	friend (male, female)
la madre	mother
el padre	father
la abuela	grandmother
el abuelo	grandfather
el bisabuelo	great-grandfather
el perro	dog
el gato	cat
la habitación	room, bedroom
los padres	parents
el huésped	lodger, boarder
el estudio	studio
la familia	family
el cuadro	painting
el retrato	portrait
la cabra	goat
el vecino, la vecina	neighbour (male, female)
cualquier cosa	anything
el hermano	brother
la hermana	sister
el constructor	builder
las gafas	glasses
los catalejos	binoculars
las herramientas	tools
(yo) me llamo	my name is (I am called)[2]
se llama	his/her/its name is
esconder	to hide
buenos días	good morning, hello (in the morning)
todo(a)	all, every
¿de quién?	whose?
antiguo(a)	old[3]
siempre	always
mucho	a lot, lots, really

Speech bubble key

●*Buenos días. Somos los amigos de María.* Good morning. We are María's friends.

●*Buenos días. Yo soy su madre.* Hello. I'm her mother.

●*Me llamo Alicia . . . y aquí está nuestro perro Guau Guau.* My name's Alicia . . . and here's our dog, Guau Guau.

●*¿De quién es el gato?* Whose cat is that?

●*Es de María. Se llama Kiti.* He's María's. His name is Kiti.

●*Aquí está la habitación de mis padres, . . . mi habitación y . . . la habitación del huésped.* Here's my parents' bedroom, . . . my room and . . . the lodger's room.

●*Aquí está el estudio de mi madre.* Here's my mother's studio.

●*Aquí escondemos todos los tesoros de la familia.* We hide all the family treasures in here.

●*Aquí está un cuadro muy viejo de la casa Salchicha.* Here's a really old painting of Salchicha house.

●*Y aquí está un retrato antiguo del abuelo de María, Santiago.* And here's an old portrait of María's grandfather, Santiago.

●*¡Oh no! Es Comelotodo, la cabra de los vecinos. Come cualquier cosa.* Oh no! It's Comelotodo, the neighbours' goat. She eats anything.

●*¿De quién es esa ropa?* Whose clothes are those?

●*Es de mi hermano . . .* They're my brother's . . .

●*y este jersey . . .* and this sweater . . .

●*Es del constructor.* It's the builder's.

●*¿De quién son estas gafas?* Whose glasses are these?

●*Son de Carmen.* They're Carmen's.

●*Me gusta esta camisa.* I like this shirt.

●*Es de Fede.* It's Fede's.

●*Me gustan mucho estos catalejos.* I really like these binoculars.

●*Son de Fede también.* They're Fede's as well.

De quién es?

Try to find these things in the picture strips and figure out whose they are. (The answer to the first one is *Este chandal es de María*.)

---

2 *Yo me llamo* comes from *llamarse* (to be called). This is a reflexive verb (see page 24). Remember that "ll" is said a bit like the "y" in "yes" (see page 4). 3 *Viejo(a)* is the usual word for "old". *Antiguo(a)* is used (for things) to mean "old" in the sense of "antique".

13

Telling people what to do

To tell someone what to do (e.g. "Wait!"), you use the imperative of the verb. Spanish has two sets of imperative forms, the *tú* and *vosotros* forms which you use to friends, and the polite *usted/ustedes* forms.[1] For most verbs, the *tú* form is the same as the *él/ella* present tense form, for example *¡Come!* (Eat!). The *vosotros* form of all verbs is made from the infinitive with its final "r" replaced by "d" for example *¡Comed!* (Eat!). The *usted/ustedes* forms are explained on page 53.

Irregular imperatives

In the *tú* form, many irregular verbs do not follow the method set out above for forming the imperative. The *tú* forms of some of the most useful irregular verbs are shown here. The *vosotros* forms are made in the usual way, so for example, the *vosotros* form of *venir* is *¡Venid!* (Come!).

tú forms

di (say)	from *decir* (to say)
haz (do)	from *hacer* (to do)
pon (put)	from *poner* (to put)
sal (go out)	from *salir* (to go out)
sé (be)	from *ser* (to be)
ten (have)	from *tener* (to have)
ven (come)	from *venir* (to come)
vete (go)	from *irse*[2] (to go, to go away)

Saying what you must do

The regular "er" verb *deber* (to have to, must) is used with the infinitive of another verb to say what you must do, for example *Debo cerrar la barrera* (I must shut the gate).

Another way, which is used even more often, is to use *tener* + *que* + the infinitive of the other verb, for example *Tengo que cerrar la barrera* (I have to shut the gate).

Hay que

Hay que is often used with the infinitive of another verb to mean "you must" in the general sense of "it is necessary to", "people have to", "one must".

1 Remember: *tú*, *vosotros*, *usted* and *ustedes* all mean "you". They are explained on page 8. **2** *Irse* is a reflexive verb. You can find out more about reflexive verbs on page 24.

14

New words

la cuerda	rope	cuidado	watch out, careful
la barrera	gate		
la cueva	cave	despacio	slowly
la lima	nail file	bueno(a)[3]	good
la cerradura	lock	venga	come on, go on
		rápido(a)	quick
lanzar	to throw	todo	everything
tirar	to pull	en	in, at
cerrar	to close, to shut	hasta luego	see you later
		ésta	this (one)
hacer compras	to do some shopping	rápidamente	quickly
		cállate, silencio	quiet, be quiet
encontrar	to find	asqueroso(a)	dirty, horrible

Directions

The imperative is very useful for giving and understanding directions. Below is a list of useful direction words:

la calle	street	girar	to turn
la carretera (principal)	(main) road	cruzar	to cross
		continuar	to carry on
el camino	path, way	seguir	to follow
la plaza	square		
la intersección	junction	primer (f: primera)	first
el semáforo	traffic lights		
el paso de peatones	pedestrian crossing	segundo(a)	second
		tercero(a)	third
		cuarto(a)	fourth
ir*	to go	todo recto	straight ahead
tomar	to take	a la izquierda	(to/on the) left
venir*	to come	a la derecha	(to/on the) right

Speech bubble key

- *¡Cuidado! Vete despacio.* Be careful! Go slowly.
- *Tranquila, Comelotodo.* (Keep) calm, Comelotodo.
- *Lanza la cuerda.* Throw the rope.
- *Sé bueno, Guau Guau.* Behave yourself (/Be good), Guau Guau.
- *¡Cuidado!* Watch out!
- *¡Venga! ¡Tirad!* Go on! Pull
- *¡Rápido, la barrera!* Quick, the gate!
- *¡Ven aquí, Comelotodo!* Come here, Comelotodo!
- *Tenéis que visitar todo – la iglesia antigua, las cuevas, Puerto Viejo . . .* You must visit everything – the old church, the caves, Puerto Viejo . . .
- *Yo tengo que hacer compras en Puerto Viejo.* I must do some shopping in Puerto Viejo.
- *Hasta luego.* See you later.
- *Hay que cerrar la barrera.* You have to shut the gate
- *Gira a la izquierda . . .* Turn left . . .
- *y toma el primer camino a la derecha.* and take the first path on the right.
- *¡Guau Guau, ven aquí!* Guau Guau, come here!
- *Ésta debe ser la casa Salchicha.* This must be the Salchicha house.
- *Debo encontrar esa pista rápidamente.* I have to find that clue fast.
- *En primer lugar tengo que buscar mi lima.* First I must look for my nail file.
- *¡Cállate!* Be quiet!
- *Estas cerraduras deben ser muy viejas.* These locks must be very old.
- *¡Cállate, perro asqueroso!* Be quiet, you horrible dog!

The way to the old church

Having taken the first path on the right, María, Fede and Carmen are here. They need five directions to get to the church. Pretend you're María and give Fede and Carmen these directions. The first is *Cruzad la carretera principal*.

(Look at the map on page 7.)

[3] The masculine adjective *bueno* shortens to *buen* when it is used before a noun.

Asking questions

There are two ways of asking questions in Spanish. You can turn a sentence, for example *Fede tiene una hermana* (Fede has got a sister), into a question just by adding two question marks (an upside-down one at the start), for example ¿*Fede tiene una hermana?* (Has Fede got a sister?). The second method is to put the subject after the verb: ¿*Tiene Fede una hermana?* (Has Fede got a sister?).[1]

Poder (to be allowed to, can, may, might)

You often use *poder* with another verb in the infinitive to ask if you can or may do something, for example ¿*Puedo mirar?* (Can/May I look?). *Poder* is a special verb called a stem-changing verb (see page 20).

Poder

yo puedo	I can
tú puedes	you can
él/ella/Ud. puede	he/she/you can
nosotros(as) podemos	we can
vosotros(as) podéis	you can
ellos(as)/Uds. pueden	they/you can

Buenas tardes, señora Salchicha.

¡Hola!

¿Tiene usted manzanas?

Quisiera dos kilos de naranjas.

¿Te gustan las fresas?

¿Puedo probar?

¿Tiene una cesta?

Son mandarinas.

Perdón, ¿puede llevar esta caja?

Question words

¿cuántos(as)?	how many?
¿cuánto(a)?	how much?
¿cómo?	how?
¿qué?	what?, which?
¿cuándo?	when?
¿dónde?	where?
¿de dónde?	where...from?, from where?
¿por qué?	why?
¿quién? (pl: ¿quiénes?)	who?
¿a qué hora?	(at) what time?

How to use question words

When you use a question word, you put it at the start followed by the verb and then the subject (as in method two given above left), for example ¿*Dónde vive Fede?* (Where does Fede live?).[2]

¿*Cuántos(as)?* (how many?) and ¿*cuánto(a)?* (how much?) change to match the noun that follows. You use ¿*cuántos?* and ¿*cuánto?* with masculine nouns, and ¿*cuántas?* and ¿*cuánta?* with feminine ones.

"Ir" verbs

So far, you have learned the present tense of regular "ar" and "er" verbs (see pages 10 and 12). The verb *vivir* (to live) shows you the present tense endings of regular "ir" verbs.

Vivir (to live)

yo vivo	I live
tú vives	you live
él/ella/Ud. vive	he/she lives, you live
nosotros(as) vivimos	we live
vosotros(as) vivís	you live
ellos(as)/Uds. viven	they/you live

¿A qué hora abre esta farmacia?

¿Qué es eso?

Farmacia Pastilla

El Mago

No lo sé. La señora Pastilla está enferma.

Perdón, ¿de dónde sale el barco para la Isla Rocosa?

Es un cangrejo.

16 1 Remember, Spanish often leaves out the word for "I", "you", "he", etc, so with either method you may end up with the same result, e.g. ¿*Tiene una hermana?* (Has he got a sister?). 2 Because you can drop "I", "you", etc, you can also make questions like ¿*Dónde vive?* (Where does he live?).

The speech bubbles at the top of the page (part of the illustration):

¿Cuántos pasteles quiere usted?

¿Qué quieres?

¿Qué sabor quieres?

Quiero un helado.

¿Cuánto valen estos pasteles?

Shopping quiz

Try saying all this in Spanish (use the *usted* form of the verb where the English has "you"):

Where is the supermarket?

I'd like an ice cream. How much do they cost?
Which flavours have you got?
I want a kilo of apples, please.
Can you carry my basket?

New words

Spanish	English	Spanish	English
la hermana	sister	probar	to taste, to try
la manzana	apple	llevar	to carry, to wear, to take
la cesta	basket		
el kilo de	kilo (of)	abrir	to open
la naranja	orange	salir*3	to leave, to go out
la mandarina	mandarin		
la fresa	strawberry	valer	to cost
la caja	box	explicar	to explain
la farmacia	chemist's, pharmacy		
el cangrejo	crab	buenas tardes	good afternoon, hello (p.m.)
el mago	magician		
el pastel	cake	(la) señora4 (Sra.)	Mrs
el sabor	flavour	(el) señor4 (Sr.)	Mr, Sir
el supermercado	supermarket	no lo sé	I don't know
la carta	letter	enfermo(a)	ill, unwell
la broma	joke	para	for
la búsqueda del tesoro	treasure hunt	de verdad	real, true

What does the letter mean?

Resting outside the church, Carmen remembers the letter the man dropped at the café . . .

¿Qué buscas Carmen?

María, ¿puedes explicar esta carta?

¿Dónde está? ¡Ah!

¿Es una broma?

María know who the writer was, and thinks she knows what and where the first clue is. Thinking about it, Fede and Carmen can figure it out too. Can you? Answer these questions and see:

¿Quién es Sancho Salchicha?
¿Qué son "los dos barcos"? (Look at the pictures on page 12.)
¿Qué habitación deben visitar María, Fede y Carmen?

¡Qué bien! ¡Es una búsqueda del tesoro de verdad!

Speech bubble key

- Buenas tardes, señora Salchicha. Hello, Mrs Salchicha.
- ¡Hola! Hello.
- ¿Tiene usted manzanas? Have you got any apples?
- ¿Tiene una cesta? Have you got a basket?
- Quisiera dos kilos de naranjas. I'd like two kilos of oranges.
- Son mandarinas. They're mandarins.
- ¿Te gustan las fresas? Do you like strawberries?
- ¿Puedo probar? May I have a taste?
- Perdón, ¿puede llevar esta caja?5 Excuse me, can you carry this box?
- ¿A qué hora abre esta farmacia? What time does this chemist's open?
- No lo sé. La señora Pastilla está enferma. I don't know. Mrs Pastilla is ill.
- Perdón, ¿de dónde sale el barco para la Isla Rocosa? Excuse me, where does the boat for Rocky Island leave from?
- ¿Qué es eso? What's that?
- Es un cangrejo. It's a crab.
- ¿Cuánto valen estos pasteles? How much do these cakes cost?
- ¿Cuántos pasteles quiere usted? How many cakes do you want?
- ¿Qué quieres? What do you want?
- Quiero un helado. I want an ice cream.
- ¿Qué sabor quieres? What flavour do you want?
- ¿Qué buscas Carmen? What are you looking for, Carmen?
- ¿Dónde está? ¡Ah! Where is it? Ah!
- María, ¿puedes explicar esta carta? María, can you explain this letter?
- ¿Es una broma? Is it a joke?
- ¡Qué bien! ¡Es una búsqueda del tesoro de verdad! Great! It's a real treasure hunt!

3 *Salir* has an irregular *yo* form: *yo salgo* (I leave). 4 When referring to someone rather than addressing them, you use *el* and *la* in front of *señor* and *señora*. 5 Notice that ¿ goes at the start of the question proper, even if this means it is halfway through a sentence.

In English, you make verbs negative by using "not", for example "I am not tired". You often also need an extra verb like "do" or "can", for example "I do not know" (or "I don't know"), rather than "I know not".

No (not)

The Spanish for "not" is *no* (which also means "no"), and it usually goes just before the verb, for example *Yo no quiero comer* (I don't want to eat). Notice how you don't need an extra verb like the English "do".

Nada, nadie, nunca

Nada, *nadie* and *nunca* mean "nothing", "nobody" and "never".

They are used before a verb. Used with *no*, they go after a verb (*no* goes just before it), and they then mean either "nothing", "nobody" and "never", or "not . . . anything", "not . . . anybody" and "not . . . ever". For example, *Nunca está enfermo* and *No está enfermo nunca* both mean "He's never ill", but the second one could also translate as "He isn't ever ill".

The Spanish for "any"

In Spanish, you don't normally use a word for "any" – you say *No hay queso* (There isn't any cheese) and *No hay libros* (There aren't any books). However, *no . . . ningún(a)* (not any) is used to underline that there are not any (at all). You use *no . . . ningún* with a masculine noun and *no . . . ninguna* with a feminine noun. The noun is always singular. For example, *No tengo ningún libro* (I haven't got any books [at all]).

Saber (to know)

Saber is a useful verb that has an irregular *yo* form: *yo sé* (I know). The other forms follow the "er" pattern (see page 12). You often use *saber* with a verb in the infinitive to mean "I know how to", "I can" (as opposed to "I'm allowed to", "I can"), for example *Sé nadar* (I can swim).

A few other verbs have an irregular *yo* form.[1] They include:

hacer (to do/make) – *yo hago* (I do/make)
poner (to put) – *yo pongo* (I put)
traer (to bring) – *yo traigo* (I bring)
ver (to see) – *yo veo* (I see)

> No es Juan, el huésped . . .

> ¿Dónde estáis? La cena está preparada.

> ¡Mirad! No son exactamente iguales.

> Ah, ya lo sé, debe ser el constructor.

> Pero el constructor no lleva traje.

> Bien, mamá. Un momento.

New words

la puerta	door	pero	but
el ladrón	burglar, thief	tan	so
el queso	cheese	fuerte	loud(ly)
el libro	book	buenas noches	good evening /night
la aspirina	aspirin		
el esparadrapo	plaster(s) (adhesive bandage)	ya (lo) sé[2]	I know
		porque	because
la cena	supper	cerrado(a)	closed, shut
las cartas	(playing) cards	a	to
el dado	die (pl: dice)	todo el mundo	everyone, everybody
la vela	candle		
el sombrero de copa	top hat	aún	yet
		fuera	outside
ladrar	to bark	preparado(a)	ready
nadar	to swim	bien	good, right, OK
traer	to bring	mamá	Mum, Mom
		un momento	one moment, just a minute
cerrado(a) con llave	locked	exactamente	exactly
		igual	(the) same

The first clue

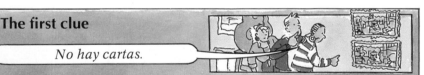

> No hay cartas.

María's family has always been puzzled by the two pictures. They did not know Sancho Salchicha had them painted when he hid his treasure. The six items missing from the second one are the clue to where to go next in the hunt. María has spotted the first item. Can you spot the other five (and make five sentences in the same way)?

María knows where to go now. Do you?

Speech bubble key

- *La puerta no está cerrada con llave . . .* The door isn't locked . . .
- *Pero las bicicletas no están ahí.* But the bicycles aren't there.
- *¡Silencio Guau Guau! No hay que ladrar tan fuerte.* Be quiet Guau Guau! You mustn't bark so loud.
- *¿Qué buscas?* What are you looking for?
- *No hay nadie.* There isn't anybody here.
- *¡Hay un ladrón en la casa!* There's a burglar in the house!
- *¿Qué barcos? No veo barcos.* What ships? I can't see any ships.
- *Buenas noches, Pedro ¡Hola, Juan!* Good evening, Pedro. Hi, Juan!
- *Buenos noches, Alicia. ¡Oh no! No hay ninguna aspirina.* Good evening, Alicia. Oh no! There aren't any aspirins.
- *Sí, ya lo sé. Es porque la farmacia está cerrada.* Yes, I know. That's because the chemist's is closed.
- *No tengo nada, no tengo aspirinas, no tengo esparadrapo.* I haven't got anything, no aspirins, no plasters.
- *¡Hola a todo el mundo!* Hi everyone!
- *¡Oh, no!, y aún no tengo la pista.* Oh no, and I haven't got the clue yet!
- *Aquí están los dos barcos.* Here are the two ships.
- *Oh, hay un hombre fuera.* Oh, there's a man outside.
- *María, ¿quién es ese hombre?* María, who's that man?
- *No sé.* I don't know.
- *No es Juan, el huésped . . .* It's not Juan, the lodger . . .
- *Ah, ya lo sé, debe ser el constructor.* Oh, I know, it must be the builder.
- *Pero el constructor no lleva traje.* But the builder doesn't wear a suit.
- *¿Dónde estáis? La cena está preparada.* Where are you? Supper's ready.
- *Bien, mamá. Un momento.* OK Mum. Just a minute.
- *¡Mirad! No son exactamente iguales.* Look! They're not exactly the same.

[2] Though *yo sé* means "I know", the expression *Ya lo sé* (literally, "I know it already" – *ya* means "already") is often used for "I know", "I know that".

Stem-changing verbs

As well as verbs of the regular "ar", "er" and "ir" patterns and irregular verbs like *ser* and *estar*, Spanish has stem-changing verbs. These are verbs that often have a change in their stem (the bit of the verb before the "ar", "er" or "ir" ending). They are otherwise regular and take the usual "ar", "er" or "ir" endings, depending on their infinitive ending.

The change occurs in all but the *nosotros* and *vosotros* forms. It happens in the stem and it is always a vowel change: "e" changes to "ie" or "i", and "o" and "u" change to "ue".[1]

To show how stem-changing verbs work, this page gives the present tense of one of each type, an "ar", "er" and "ir" stem-changing verb, and an example of each stem change ("e" to "ie", "e" to "i" and "o" to "ue").[2]

Pensar (ie) (to think)

yo pienso	I think (am thinking)
tú piensas	you think
él/ella/Ud. piensa	he/she thinks, you think
nosotros(as) pensamos	we think
vosotros(as) pensáis	you think
ellos(as)/Uds. piensan	they/you think

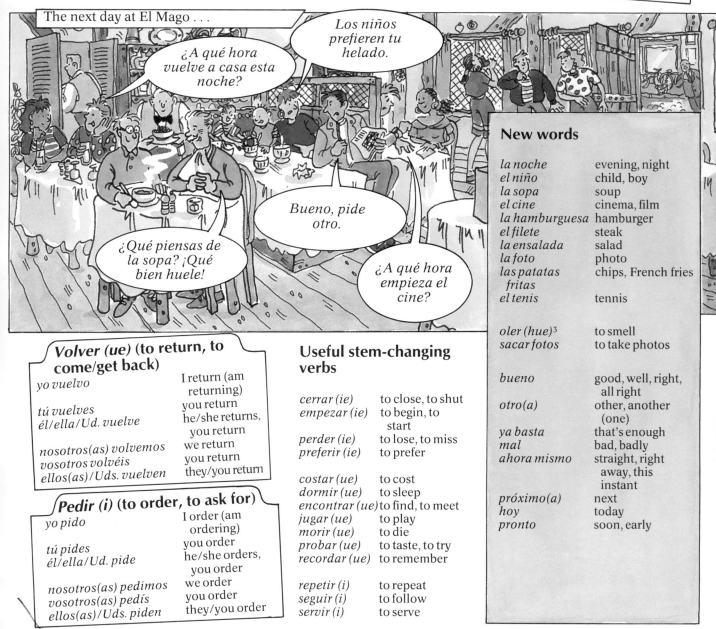

The next day at El Mago . . .

¿A qué hora vuelve a casa esta noche?

Los niños prefieren tu helado.

¿Qué piensas de la sopa? ¡Qué bien huele!

Bueno, pide otro.

¿A qué hora empieza el cine?

New words

la noche	evening, night
el niño	child, boy
la sopa	soup
el cine	cinema, film
la hamburguesa	hamburger
el filete	steak
la ensalada	salad
la foto	photo
las patatas fritas	chips, French fries
el tenis	tennis
oler (hue)[3]	to smell
sacar fotos	to take photos
bueno	good, well, right, all right
otro(a)	other, another (one)
ya basta	that's enough
mal	bad, badly
ahora mismo	straight, right away, this instant
próximo(a)	next
hoy	today
pronto	soon, early

Volver (ue) (to return, to come/get back)

yo vuelvo	I return (am returning)
tú vuelves	you return
él/ella/Ud. vuelve	he/she returns, you return
nosotros(as) volvemos	we return
vosotros volvéis	you return
ellos(as)/Uds. vuelven	they/you return

Pedir (i) (to order, to ask for)

yo pido	I order (am ordering)
tú pides	you order
él/ella/Ud. pide	he/she orders, you order
nosotros(as) pedimos	we order
vosotros(as) pedís	you order
ellos(as)/Uds. piden	they/you order

Useful stem-changing verbs

cerrar (ie)	to close, to shut
empezar (ie)	to begin, to start
perder (ie)	to lose, to miss
preferir (ie)	to prefer
costar (ue)	to cost
dormir (ue)	to sleep
encontrar (ue)	to find, to meet
jugar (ue)	to play
morir (ue)	to die
probar (ue)	to taste, to try
recordar (ue)	to remember
repetir (i)	to repeat
seguir (i)	to follow
servir (i)	to serve

1 Only a few verbs have an "u" that changes to "ue". *Jugar* (to play) is the most useful one. **2** From now on, word lists in this book show stem-changing verbs followed by a bracketed "ie", "i" or "ue". This tells you that the verb is stem-changing and

Speech bubble key

- *¿A qué hora vuelve a casa esta noche?* What time is he getting home this evening?
- *Los niños prefieren tu helado.* The children prefer your ice cream.
- *Bueno, pide otro.* All right, get me another one.
- *¿Qué piensas de la sopa? ¡Qué bien huele!*[3] What do you think of the soup? It smells great! (How good it smells!)

- *¿A qué hora empieza el cine?* What time does the film start?
- *Quiere queso.* She wants cheese.
- *¿Te gustan las hamburguesas?* Do you like hamburgers?
- *Sí, pero prefiero el filete.* Yes, but I prefer steak.
- *¡Agh! ¡Qué mal sirven la ensalada!* Ugh! What bad salad they serve! (How badly they serve salad!)
- *¿Qué hacen esos niños?* What are

those children doing?
- *¿Y por qué sacan fotos?* And why are they taking photos?
- *Cuidado, trae la sopa.* Watch out, he's bringing some soup.
- *¡Bueno, ya basta! Salid ahora mismo.* Right, that's enough! Get out this instant.
- *¡Hey, venga!* Hey, come on!
- *¡Mirad, tengo la próxima pista!* Look, I've got the next clue!

Crossword puzzle

Each solution is one or more Spanish words. The words you need are shown in English in the brackets. Put them in the correct form for the Spanish sentence and they should slot into the puzzle.

Across
1. *Él* (prefers) *patatas fritas.* (8)
2. (Yes), *quiero queso.* (2)
3. *¿A qué hora empieza el cine* (today)? (3)
7. *Tengo* (a) (*gato*). (2)

8. *Quisiera* (tea). (2)
10. *¿Te gusta la* (soup)? (4)
11. *¿Cuánto cuesta un* (ice cream)? (6)
12. (The) *chicos están en el café.* (3)

Down
1. *Tenemos la* (clue). (5)
4. (We close) *pronto.* (8)
5. *¿A qué hora* (get back) *tú a casa?* (7)
6. *¿Por qué sacan* (photos)? (5)
9. *Me gusta* (to play) *al tenis.* (5)

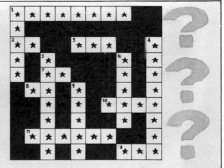

Trace the crossword outline onto a piece of paper but leave out the stars. They show the squares you have to fill.

what the stem vowel changes to. **3** *Oler* (to smell) is stem-changing ("o" becomes "ue"), but it also adds an "h" on the front of "ue".

Prepositions

Prepositions are words like "in", "on" or "of". Most Spanish ones are easy to use, for example *Tu jersey está en tu habitación* (Your sweater's in your room). Here are the most common ones:

a	to, at (for time)
al lado de	by, next to
ante	before, in front of
cerca de	close to, near
con	with
contra	against
de	of, from, by
debajo de	under, underneath
delante de	in front of
dentro de	inside
desde	from, since
detrás de	behind
en	in, at, on
encima de	on, over
enfrente de	opposite
entre	between, among
fuera de	outside
hacia	toward, about
hasta	until
junto a	next to
lejos de	far from
para	for, toward, to
por	for (because of), through, along
según	according to
sin	without
sobre	above, over, on, on top of
tras	after

De and a

Remember that with *el*, *de* becomes *del*. *De* is used to say whose something is (see page 12), but also in lots of other ways, for example *Soy de España* (I'm from Spain). *A* also joins up with *el*, for example *Voy al café* (I'm going to the café). With prepositions that end in *de* or *a* such as *cerca de*, *de* and *a* behave in the same way, so you say *cerca del café* (near the café).

Choosing the right preposition

Beware: Spanish does not always use the same preposition as English. For instance, to say "on" a bus, train or plane, Spanish uses "in" (*en*). It also uses *en* to say "by" bus, train or plane.

Ir and venir

These are two useful irregular verbs.

Ir (to go)

yo voy	I go
tú vas	you go
él/ella/Ud. va	he/she goes, you go
nosotros(as) vamos	we go
vosotros(as) vais	you go
ellos(as)/Uds. van	they/you go

Venir (to come)

yo vengo	I come
tú vienes	you come
él/ella/Ud. viene	he/she comes, you come
nosotros(as) venimos	we come
vosotros(as) venís	you come
ellos(as)/Uds. vienen	they/you come

Ten minutes later . . .

New words

España	Spain	*la respuesta*	answer
la ventana	window	*la pregunta*	question
la salida	exit	*la vaca*	cow
la mujer	woman	*la colina*	hill
el jardín	garden	*el árbol*	tree
la fuente	fountain		
el muelle	quay, dock	*el mismo, la*	the (very) same
la red	net	*misma, los*	
la nota	note	*mismos, las*	
el banco	bench, bank	*mismas*	
la lupa	magnifying glass	*rápido*	quick, quickly
el compañero, la	mate, good friend	*calvo(a)*	bald
compañera	(male, female)	*allí*	(over) there
el colegio	school	*de prisa*	quick, quickly
el desván	attic	*bien*	good, right, OK,
el edificio	building		well

The clue from the inn

La próxima pista está en un edificio en Puerto Viejo. Buscad las respuestas a estas preguntas:
¿Dónde está la vaca?
¿Dónde está el perro?
¿Dónde está el banco?
¿Dónde está la granja?

When María's friend finally finds his magnifying glass, Fede, Carmen and María read the note that Fede found in the inn. They have to answer four questions. Luckily the photo María took of the painted seat holds the answers. Can you figure out the four answers (in Spanish)?

Now can you figure out which building they have to go to and finish Carmen's sentence? (The four answers apply to only one building in Puerto Viejo.)

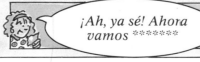

¡Ah, ya sé! Ahora vamos ******

Speech bubble key

- *¡Mirad por la ventana!* Look through the window!
- *Cerca de la salida . . . junto a la mujer alta.* Near the exit . . . next to the tall woman.
- *¡Es el hombre del aeropuerto!* It's the man from the airport!
- *¡Es el hombre con la carta!* It's the man with the letter!
- *¡Es el hombre del jardín!* It's the man from the garden!
- *¡Es el mismo hombre!* It's the same man!
- *¡Rápido! Debe querer nuestro tesoro.* Quickly! He must want our treasure.
- *¡Oh no! ¡El hombre calvo! Allí, delante de la fuente.* Oh no! The bald man! There, in front of the fountain.
- *Viene por el muelle.* He's coming along the quay.
- *¡De prisa, venid detrás de esta red!* Quick, come behind this net!
- *¡Está bien!* It's OK!
- *Bien, pon la nota y las fotos en este banco.* Right, put the note and the photos on this bench.
- *¿Tienes una lupa?* Have you got a magnifying glass?
- *Sí, pero está en casa.* Yes, but it's at home.
- *¡Ah, ya sé! Podemos ir a casa de Rafa.* Ah, I know! We can go to Rafa's.
- *Rafa es un compañero. Vive enfrente de la estación.* Rafa's a mate. He lives opposite the station.
- *Sí, tengo una lupa. Está encima de la mesa en el desván.* Yes, I've got a magnifying glass. It's on the table in the attic.

Reflexive verbs, "who" and "which"

Reflexive verbs are verbs whose infinitive ends with *se* and whose present tense begins with a word like *me* (myself) or *te* (yourself) – see *levantarse* below. They can be regular, stem-changing or irregular.[1] Some of them seem logical as they are an action you do to yourself (*afeitarse* – to shave), but many are reflexive for no clear reason (*terminarse* – to end, to finish). English has no real equivalent.[2]

> ¿Por qué os escondéis?

> Porque no nos gusta el colegio.

Levantarse (to get up)

yo me levanto	I get up
tú te levantas	you get up
él/ella/Ud. se levanta	he/she gets up, you get up
nosotros(as) nos levantamos	we get up
vosotros(as) os levantáis	you get up
ellos(as)/Uds. se levantan	they/you get up

The imperative is made in the usual way (see page 14), but you attach *te* to the *tú* form and *os* to the *vosotros* form (minus "d"), so you say *Levántate* and *Levantaos* (Get up).

> ¿Qué hora es?

> Son las ocho, señorita.

> ¿Y ahora?

> Son las nueve y cuarto.

¿Qué hora es?

To answer *¿Qué hora es?* (What time is it?, What's the time?), you say *Es la una* (It is one [o'clock])[3] and, for all other times, *Son las . . .* (It is . . .):

dos/tres	two/three (o'clock)
seis (de la mañana)	six (in the morning)
. . . de la tarde	. . . in the afternoon
. . . de la noche	. . . in the evening
dos y cuarto/media	(a) quarter/half past two
dos menos cuarto	a quarter to two
dos y diez/veinte	ten/twenty past two
dos menos diez/veinte	ten/twenty to two
(es) mediodía/medianoche	(it's) midday/midnight

To answer *¿A qué hora?* (What time? as in "What time's your train?") put *a* (at) in front of the time, for example *A la una* (At one [o'clock]).

> Gaspar, ¿a qué hora te levantas?

> A las siete y media.

> ¿Te vistes solo?

> Claro.

> No me siento bien.

> ¡Bien, cálmate!

"Who" and "which"

English can use these words as a verb's subject (The girl who/The book which is there) or direct object (The girl who(m)[4]/The book which I'm looking for). "Who(m)" refers to a person, "which" to a thing. Note that we often say "that" instead, or we just drop the word (The girl I'm looking for).

Spanish is simpler. To refer to a person or thing, you normally use *que* for the subject and the object, so you say *La chica/El libro que está allí* and *La chica/El libro que busco*, and *que* is never left out. After a preposition, though, you use *quien* to refer to a person and *quienes* (the plural) to refer to people (*La chica con quien hablo* – The girl with who(m) I'm talking).

> ¡Mira! Es el lápiz que falta.

> ¡Eh! Ese dibujo que tienes es de Manuel.

---

24   1 Regular and stem-changing reflexive verbs follow the pattern shown by the bit of their infinitive ending in front of *-se* ("ar", "er" or "ir"). 2 Many verbs are used either as a normal verb or as a reflexive, e.g. *romper* means "to break (something)", but *romperse* means "to break" as in "The cup broke". 3 Numbers are shown on page 58. 4 Note that "whom" is better English

Speech bubble key

- *Por qué os escondéis?* Why are you hiding?
- *Porque no nos gusta el colegio.* Because we don't like school.
- *¿Qué hora es?* What's the time?
- *Son las ocho, señorita.* It's eight o'clock, Miss.
- *¿Y ahora?* And now?
- *Son las nueve y cuarto.* It's a quarter past nine.
- *¡Gaspar! ¿A qué hora te levantas?* Gaspar, what time do you get up?
- *A las siete y media.* At half past seven.
- *¿Te vistes solo?* Do you get dressed on your own?
- *Claro.* Of course.
- *No me siento bien.* I don't feel well.
- *¡Bien, cálmate!* Right, calm down!
- *¡Mira! Es el lápiz que falta.* Look! That's the crayon that's missing.
- *¡Eh! Ese dibujo que tienes es de Manuel.* Hey! That drawing (which) you've got is Manuel's.
- *¡Oh! Esa debe ser la pista que buscamos.* Oh! That must be the clue (that) we're looking for.
- *Mira esa foto antigua.* Look at that old photo.
- *El hombre que corta la cinta es Sancho Salchicha.* The man (who's) cutting the ribbon is Sancho Salchicha.
- *Y aquí está la señal que se encuentra en todas sus pistas.* And there's the sign that's on all his clues.
- *Podemos volver esta tarde.* We can come back this evening.
- *¡Buena idea!* Good idea!

New words

el día	day	faltar	to be missing
el lápiz[5] (de colores)	crayon	cortar	to cut
el dibujo	drawing	encontrarse (ue)	to be (found/ situated)
la cinta	ribbon	volver (ue)	to come back, to
la señal	sign		return
la tarde	afternoon, evening	pasarlo muy bien[6]	to have (lots of) fun
la idea	idea	tomar prestado[7]	to borrow
la postal	postcard	lavarse	to wash (yourself)
afeitarse	to shave	despertarse (ie)	to wake up
terminarse	to end, to finish	acostarse (ue)	to go to bed
esconderse	to hide		
vestirse (i)	to dress, to get dressed	claro	of course
sentirse (ie) bien/mal	to feel well/not well	precioso(a)	lovely, beautiful
		simpático(a)	nice
calmarse	to calm down	o	or
hablar	to talk, to speak	(muchos) besos	(lots of) kisses

A postcard from Carmen

While they wait for school to end so they can take a closer look at the old photo, Carmen sends a postcard home. Read it and see if you can answer the questions. (Give full sentence answers in Spanish.)

> *Querida mamá:*
>
> *Lo pasamos muy bien. La casa es preciosa y los padres de María son muy amables. Tienen también un huésped muy simpático, Juan, un perro y un gato, y unos vecinos que tienen una cabra. Hay bicicletas que podemos tomar prestadas. Dormimos en las tiendas de campaña (que están en el jardín), pero comemos y nos lavamos en la casa. Me despierto a las seis de la mañana porque el sol brilla y los pájaros cantan, pero Fede se despierta a las ocho. Nos acostamos a las nueve y media o a las diez. ¿Te gusta esta postal? Es de Puerto Viejo.*
>
> *Muchos besos,*
> *Carmen*

Señora Ana M
Calle Mayor n
Madrid 3702

¿Quién tiene una cabra?
¿Dónde duermen Carmen y Fede?

¿A qué hora se despierta Carmen?
¿A qué hora se despierta Fede?
¿A qué hora se acuestan?

for the object. **5** Plural: *los lápices.* **6** Literally, "to pass it well". *Lo* goes before the verb except in the infinitive, e.g. *Lo paso muy bien* (I'm having fun). **7** *Prestado* agrees like an adjective with whatever you are borrowing.

Saying what you are doing

English has two present tenses (as in "I walk" and "I am walking"). Spanish also has two, and so far you have learned the simple "I walk" type. The "I am walking" sort, called the present progressive, is not used as much as in English. Spanish uses it to make clear that you are doing something right now.

The present progressive

To make the present progressive you use *estar* (see page 8) + the "-ing" form of the verb you need. This is made by adding -*ando* to the stem of "ar" verbs (so *estoy andando* is "I am walking"), and – *iendo* to the stem of "er" and "ir" verbs (*estoy comiendo/ viviendo* – I am eating/living).[1]

¿Quién es usted? ¿Qué está haciendo aquí?

Eh . . . soy el técnico, estoy arreglando la fotocopiadora.

Entonces, ¿funciona bien ahora?

Eh, sí . . .

Sí, estoy envolviendo una parte que está rota.

¿Puedo cerrar, señor López?

Sí, claro.

Porque and por

Porque means "because", for example *Quiero un jersey nuevo porque este jersey es muy feo* (I want a new sweater because this sweater's really ugly). For "because of", you use *por*, for instance *Estoy aquí por María* (I'm here because of María).

Para (in order to, to)

Para can mean "for" (see page 22), but is also used with a verb in the infinitive to mean "in order to", "so as to", "to", for example *Van al colegio para buscar una pista* (They go to the school to look for a clue).

¿Qué podemos hacer para entrar?

¡Venid por aquí!

¿Qué estás haciendo, Carmen?

No seas tonto . . .

Estoy buscando la foto porque ya no está en la pared.

¡Demasiado tarde! El hombre calvo tiene la pista.

¿Cómo lo sabes?

Porque ése es su maletín.

Bien, debemos llevar esto a la comisaría.

Verbs with people

In Spanish, you put *a* between a verb and its direct or indirect object if this is a person (or a pet animal), for example *Visito a María* (I'm visiting María).

Saber and conocer

Saber (see page 18) means "to know" in the sense of "know how to" or "know that . . .". For "to know" meaning "be acquainted with" (people, films, books and so on), Spanish has another verb, *conocer*. Like *saber*, *conocer* has an irregular *yo* form, *conozco* (I know). Otherwise it follows the "er" pattern shown on page 12. *Reconocer* (to recognize) behaves in the same way.

---

1 The only exceptions are *ir*, *poder* and *venir*, whose "-ing" forms are *yendo*, *pudiendo* and *viniendo*, and all "ir" stem-changing verbs. With these, "e" and "o" in the stem change to "i" and "u", e.g. *dormir*, *durmiendo*; *pedir*, *pidiendo*.

New words

el técnico	mechanic, technician	*roto(a)*	broken
la fotocopiadora	photocopier	*entonces*	so
la parte	part, share	*nuevo(a)*	new
la pared	wall	*feo(a)*	ugly
la comisaría	police station	*por aquí*	this way, around here
el policía	policeman[2]		
la máquina	machine	*tonto(a)*	stupid, daft
		ya	any more, already
		demasiado	too
arreglar	to repair, to mend	*tarde*	late
envolver (ue)	to wrap up	*lo*	it[3]
encontrar (ue)	to find	*ése*	that (one)
funcionar	to work, to function	*esto*	this
entrar	to go in, to enter	*mañana por la mañana*	tomorrow morning
reconocer *	to recognize		
pensar (ie)	to think	*bastante*	quite
trabajar	to work	*difícil*	difficult

Mix and match

Here are two sets of six sentences. Each sentence from the first set can be joined to one from the second set using *porque* or *para*. Can you figure out what the six new sentences are? (You should use *para* in the two cases where it is possible. When you do, you must drop the first word from the second sentence.)

No podemos ir ahora.
Me llevo la bicicleta.
Conocemos a la señora Pastilla.
¡Silencio! Tengo que pensar.
Va a Villatorres.
El técnico está aquí.

Quiere hacer compras.
Es muy difícil.
Quiero ir a Puerto Viejo.
Trabaja en la farmacia.
La máquina está rota.
Estamos comiendo.

Speech bubble key

- *¿Quién es usted? ¿Qué está haciendo aquí?* Who are you? What are you doing here?
- *Eh . . . soy el técnico, estoy arreglando la fotocopiadora. Er . . .* I'm the mechanic. I'm just repairing the photocopier.
- *Sí, estoy envolviendo una parte que está rota.* Yes, I'm just wrapping up a part that's broken.
- *Entonces, ¿funciona bien ahora?* So, it's OK now?
- *Eh, sí . . .* Er, yes . . .
- *¿Puedo cerrar, señor López?* Can I close up, Mr López?
- *Sí, claro.* Yes, of course.
- *¿Qué podemos hacer para entrar?* What do we do to get in?
- *¡Venid por aquí!* Come this way!
- *¿Qué estás haciendo, Carmen?* What are you doing, Carmen?
- *No seas tonto . . .* Don't be stupid . . .
- *Estoy buscando la foto porque ya no está en la pared.* I'm looking for the photo because it's not on the wall any more.
- *¡Demasiado tarde! El hombre calvo tiene la pista.* Too late! The bald man's got the clue.
- *¿Cómo lo sabes?* How do you know (it)?
- *Porque ése es su maletín.* Because that's his briefcase.
- *Bien, debemos llevar esto a la comisaría.* Right, we should take this to the police station.
- *Está cerrada.* It's closed.
- *Bien, tenemos que volver mañana por la mañana.* Right, we must come back tomorrow morning.
- *¿Conoces al policía?* Do you know the policeman?
- *Sí, es bastante simpático.* Yes, he's quite nice.

---

2 For "policewoman", you normally say *la agente de policía*. *La policía* is also possible, but generally means "the police".
3 You already know three expressions that use *lo*: *No lo sé* (I don't know [it]), *Yo lo sé* (I know [it]) and *Lo paso muy bien* (I'm having fun). You will find out more about *lo* on page 28.

Personal pronouns

Personal pronouns are words like "I", "you" and so on. When they are the object of a verb, some of them change, for example "I" becomes "me". In English, the word is the same for a direct or an indirect object: you say "He watches me" and "He passes the book to me" (or "passes me the book"). In Spanish, the pronoun may have different forms (see right).

subject	direct object	indirect object
yo (I)	*me* (me)	*me* ([to] me)
tú (you)	*te* (you)	*te* ([to] you)
él (he)	*lo* (him/it)[1]	*le* ([to] him/it)[1]
ella (she)	*la* (her/it)[1]	*le* ([to] her/it)[1]
usted (you)	*lo/la* (you)	*le* ([to] you)
nosotros(as) (we)	*nos* (us)	*nos* ([to] us)
vosotros(as) (you)	*os* (you)	*os* ([to] you)
ellos (they)	*los* (them)	*les* ([to] them)
ellas (they)	*las* (them)	*les* ([to] them)
ustedes (you)	*los/las* (you)	*les* ([to] you)

Word order

Spanish personal pronouns usually go before the verb, as in *Me mira* (He watches me). With the present progressive, though, the object pronouns can go before the verb or on the end of the *-ndo* form: *Me está mirando* OR *Está mirándome* (He's watching me). You have a similar choice if you use a main verb plus an infinitive verb: *La quiere encontrar* OR *Quiere encontrarla* (He wants to find it).

If you use a direct and an indirect object pronoun, the indirect one comes first (*Me lo enseña* – He shows it to me). If both pronouns begin with "l", the indirect object pronoun (either *le* or *les*) changes to *se*, for example *Se lo enseña* (He shows it to them).

¿Qué hacemos con el maletín?

¿Se lo enseñamos a tus padres?

No, no debemos enseñárselo.

Primero debemos contar todo a la policía.

Lo puedo esconder en mi tienda de campaña.

La cena está preparada.

¡Buena idea!

Personal pronouns with imperatives

With an imperative verb, any object pronoun goes on the end of the verb, for example *¡Enseñadme la pista!* (Show me the clue!) or *¡Enseñádmela!*[2] (Show it to me!). With *no* and an imperative verb, though, you put the pronoun(s) between *no* and the verb (*¡No me la enseñes!* Don't show it to me!).

Pronouns after "in", "on", etc.

If you use a preposition (a word like "in", "on" or "for" – see page 22) with a personal pronoun after it, as in "The sweater's for me", you use the subject pronouns except that *mí* replaces *yo* and *ti* replaces *tú*. So you say *El jersey es para mí.*[3]

After dinner . . .

El hombre calvo tiene la pista del colegio.

Para encontrarla, hay que buscar al hombre calvo.

Su dirección puede estar en el maletín.

Acércate.

---

28 **1** Remember, Spanish does not use a word for "it" as a subject. It uses the verb alone, e.g. *Está aquí* (It's here). For "it" as a direct object, you use *lo* to refer to a masculine noun and *la* for a feminine noun, e.g. referring to *el jersey* (jumper): *Lo tengo* (I've got it); referring to *la carta* (map): *La tengo*. The indirect object "it" is always *le*. **2** The stressed syllable in *enseñad* is

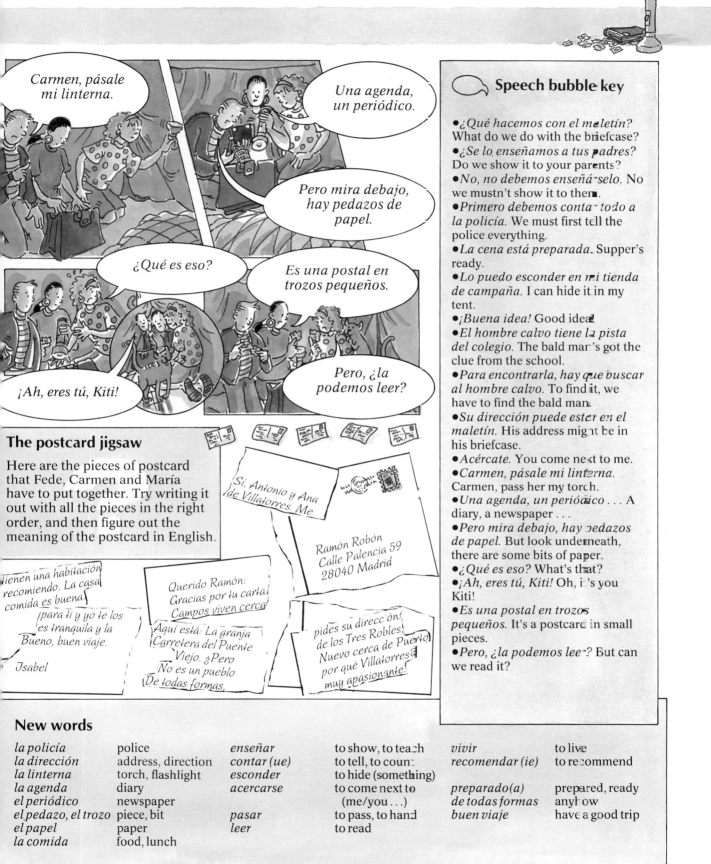

The postcard jigsaw

Here are the pieces of postcard that Fede, Carmen and María have to put together. Try writing it out with all the pieces in the right order, and then figure out the meaning of the postcard in English.

Postcard pieces:

Sí, Antonio y Ana de Villatorres. Me

*Ramón Robón
Calle Palencia 59
28040 Madrid*

Tienen una habitación recomiendo. La casa comida es buena.

para ti y yo te los es tranquila y la Bueno, buen viaje.

Isabel

*Querido Ramón:
Gracias por tu carta. Campos viven cerca*

Aquí está: La granja Carretera del Puente Viejo. ¿Pero No es un pueblo De todas formas,

pides su dirección de los Tres Robles Nuevo cerca de Puerto por qué Villatorres muy apasionante!

Speech bubble key

- *¿Qué hacemos con el maletín?* What do we do with the briefcase?
- *¿Se lo enseñamos a tus padres?* Do we show it to your parents?
- *No, no debemos enseñárselo.* No we mustn't show it to them.
- *Primero debemos contar todo a la policía.* We must first tell the police everything.
- *La cena está preparada.* Supper's ready.
- *Lo puedo esconder en mi tienda de campaña.* I can hide it in my tent.
- *¡Buena idea!* Good idea!
- *El hombre calvo tiene la pista del colegio.* The bald man's got the clue from the school.
- *Para encontrarla, hay que buscar al hombre calvo.* To find it, we have to find the bald man.
- *Su dirección puede estar en el maletín.* His address might be in his briefcase.
- *Acércate.* You come next to me.
- *Carmen, pásale mi linterna.* Carmen, pass her my torch.
- *Una agenda, un periódico . . .* A diary, a newspaper . . .
- *Pero mira debajo, hay pedazos de papel.* But look underneath, there are some bits of paper.
- *¿Qué es eso?* What's that?
- *¡Ah, eres tú, Kiti!* Oh, it's you Kiti!
- *Es una postal en trozos pequeños.* It's a postcard in small pieces.
- *Pero, ¿la podemos leer?* But can we read it?

New words

la policía	police
la dirección	address, direction
la linterna	torch, flashlight
la agenda	diary
el periódico	newspaper
el pedazo, el trozo	piece, bit
el papel	paper
la comida	food, lunch
enseñar	to show, to teach
contar (ue)	to tell, to count
esconder	to hide (something)
acercarse	to come next to (me/you . . .)
pasar	to pass, to hand
leer	to read
vivir	to live
recomendar (ie)	to recommend
preparado(a)	prepared, ready
de todas formas	anyhow
buen viaje	have a good trip

"ñad" (see rules on stress, page 5). When *me* and *la* are added, a stress mark is also added on "ñad" (which turns into "ñád") to keep the stress there. **3** If you want to use *mí* or *ti* after *con* (with), the words join up and you add "go" on the end, so you say *conmigo* (with me) and *contigo* (with you).

Past tenses and adverbs

So far, you have learned verbs in the present tense. From here to page 39, you will learn about past tenses. These are for talking about the past (e.g. "did", "was doing", "has done"). Like English, Spanish has many past tenses – one of these is called the imperfect.

The imperfect tense of *ser*, *estar* and *tener*

The three most useful verbs to learn in the imperfect are *tener*, *ser* and *estar*. For them, the imperfect is the most commonly used past tense.

Tener (imperfect tense)

tenía[1]	I had/was having/used to have
tenías	you had
tenía	he/she/you had
teníamos	we had
teníais	you had
tenían	they/you had

Ser/estar (imperfect tense)

era/estaba[1]	I was/was being/used to be
eras/estabas	you were
era/estaba	he/she/it was, you were
éramos/estábamos	we were
erais/estabais	you were
eran/estaban	they/you were

The next morning . . .

Entonces, ¿dónde estaba este maletín?

Estaba encima de la fotocopiadora del colegio.

¿Y por qué estabais vosotros tú allí?

Porque estamos buscando un tesoro . . .

y había una pista en el colegio.

¿Qué tesoro?

Es de mi familia.

Ah, ya entiendo, y este estafador lo quiere robar . . .

¡Exactamente! La pista es una foto antigua.

Ayer por la noche la foto ya no estaba allí . . .

pero el maletín del estafador estaba allí.

Probablemente es el maletín del maestro.

No, el estafador lo tenía antes.

¡Ya basta! Ahora regresad a casa.

Adverbs

These are words like "slowly" that give extra meaning to a verb. There are various types, for instance adverbs of time (that say when something happens), or of place (where it happens), or of manner (how it happens). Spanish adverbs of manner are easy to spot as many end in *-mente*. They are made by adding *-mente* to an adjective (to its feminine form if it has one), for example *realmente* (really), *exactamente* (exactly).

Useful adverbs

Time

a menudo	often
antes	before
antes de ayer, anteayer	the day before yesterday
ayer	yesterday
ayer por la noche, anoche	yesterday/last night
ayer por la tarde	yesterday evening
de vez en cuando, a veces	sometimes
entonces	then, so
habitualmente	usually, normally[2]
hoy	today
mañana	tomorrow
pasado mañana	the day after tomorrow
siempre	always
todavía, aún	still[3]
ya	already, now, yet[4]

Place

ahí	there
allí, allá	(over) there
aquí	here
en alguna parte	somewhere
en ninguna parte	nowhere
en/por todas partes	everywhere
por aquí	over/around here

Manner

afortunadamente, felizmente	luckily, fortunately, happily
casi	almost, nearly
exactamente	exactly
fuerte	strongly, loudly
mal	badly
por fortuna	luckily
probablemente, seguramente	probably
realmente	really
tal vez, quizá	maybe, perhaps

1 From now on, the words *yo, tú, él*, etc. are left out of verb tables in this book. This is because, once you know these words well, it is easiest to learn Spanish verbs without them. **2** Note that the most common way of talking about something that you usually do is to use the verb *soler (ue)* (to be used to/in the habit of) + an infinitive verb, e.g. *Suelo llegar a las seis* (I usually

New words

la familia	family	devolver (ue)	to bring/take back
el estafador	crook	seguir (i)	to follow, to carry
el maestro	teacher		on, to continue
el bolsillo	pocket		
el restaurante	restaurant	ya basta	it's/that's enough
		¡qué le vamos a	too bad!
había[5]	there was/were	hacer!	
entender (ie)	to understand	bonito(a)	pretty
robar	to steal, to rob	caro(a)	expensive
regresar	to come/go (back)		

Speech bubble key

- *Entonces, ¿dónde estaba este maletín?* So, where was this briefcase?
- *Estaba encima de la fotocopiadora del colegio.* It was on the school photocopier
- *¿Y por qué estabais vosotros allí?* And why were you there?
- *Porque estamos buscando un tesoro . . .* Because we're looking for treasure . . .
- *y había una pista en el colegio.* and there was a clue in the school.
- *¿Qué tesoro?* What treasure?
- *Es de mi familia.* It belongs to my family.
- *Ah, ya entiendo, y este estafador lo quiere robar . . .* Ah, I see (now), and this crook wants to steal it . . .
- *¡Exactamente! La pista es una foto antigua.* Exactly! The clue is an old photo.
- *Ayer por la noche la foto ya no estaba allí . . .* The photo wasn't there any more last night . . .
- *pero el maletín del estafador estaba allí.* but the crook's briefcase was there.
- *Probablemente es el maletín del maestro.* It's probably the teacher's briefcase.
- *No, el estafador lo tenía antes.* No, the crook had it before.
- *¡Ya basta! Ahora regresad a casa.* That's enough! Go home now.
- *Devuelve este maletín al colegio ahora mismo.* Take this briefcase back to the school right away.
- *¡Qué le vamos a hacer! Tenemos que seguir sin la policía.* Too bad! We have to carry on without the police.
- *Por fortuna sabemos la dirección del hombre calvo.* Luckily, we know the bald man's address.
- *¡Oh, mirad! Todavía tengo la agenda que estaba en el maletín.* Oh look! I've still got the diary that was in the briefcase.
- *Estaba en mi bolsillo.* It was in my pocket.

Picture puzzle

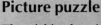

The girl in the pink shirt is showing her friend some photos of a recent trip to the seaside. Can you match the six things she says with the right photos?

1 *Nuestro hotel era pequeño y simpático.*
2 *Había un jardín muy grande.*
3 *La playa estaba muy cerca del hotel.*
4 *Yo tenía una habitación muy bonita.*
5 *Mis padres estaban realmente cansados.*
6 *Los restaurantes no eran muy caros.*

get up at six). **3** Used with *no*, *todavía* and *aún* both mean "not . . . yet". **4** Used with *no*, *ya* means "not . . . any more". **5** *Había* is the imperfect of *hay* (there is/are).

The imperfect tense

The Spanish imperfect tense has two main uses.[1] It is used for things that were happening – where, for example, you would say "I was cycling". It is also used for things that used to happen often, such as "I cycled to school every day". Note that English can say the same thing (I cycled) for things that happened often and for a once-only past event – "I cycled to school every day" and "I cycled to school that day" – but Spanish uses different tenses, the imperfect for things that happened often, and the preterite for once-only past events (see page 34).

How to form the imperfect tense

To form the imperfect tense of nearly all Spanish verbs, you take the stem (the infinitive minus the "ar", "er" or "ir" ending), and you add one of two sets of imperfect tense endings.

For "ar" verbs, you add the endings -aba, -abas, -aba, -abamos, -abais and -aban, for example yo andaba (I was walking/walked [often]). For "er" and "ir" verbs, the endings are -ía, -ías, -ía, -íamos, -íais and -ían, for example yo comía (I was eating/ate [often]) and yo vivía (I was living/lived [often]).

Stem-changing verbs behave like normal "ar", "er" and "ir" verbs in the imperfect – they do not have a stem-change and take the endings shown below left.

Irregular verbs in the imperfect tense

Only three Spanish verbs are irregular in the imperfect tense: ser (to be – see its imperfect on page 30), ir (to go) and ver (to see). All other verbs form the imperfect as explained above, even if they are irregular in other tenses. The imperfect of ir and ver are shown here.

Ir (imperfect tense)

iba	I was going/went (often)
ibas	you were going
iba	he/she/it was going, you were going
íbamos	we were going
ibais	you were going
iban	they/you were going

Ver (imperfect tense)

veía	I was seeing/saw (often)
veías	you were seeing
veía	he/she/it was seeing
veíamos	we were seeing
veíais	you were seeing
veían	they/you were seeing

¿Qué es eso?

Estaba en la agenda.

Parece interesante . . .

Pájaros en extinción en las islas Lorazul

Hace cien años, había muchos loros azules en las islas Lorazul. Los habitantes los adoraban y construían templos para ellos. Estos pájaros ahora están en extinción y está prohibido capturarlos. El año pasado, de vez en cuando se podía ver alguno en Kuku, una isla desierta remota.

Señor Robón:
Encuéntreme una pareja de loros azules para mi colección. Su remuneración: 3 millones de pesetas.

Señora Buitre

1 You already know the imperfect tense of a few verbs (see page 30).

> ¡Eh! Las islas Lorazul... Mi bisabuelo iba a menudo allí para estudiar las plantas.

> Era botánico...

> Y el hombre calvo estaba en esas islas para robar loros.

> Venid, os quiero enseñar una cosa en casa.

Speech bubble key

- *¿Qué es eso?* What's that?
- *Estaba en la agenda.* It was in the diary.
- *Parece interesante...* It looks interesting...

The magazine cutting:
Endangered birds on the Lorazul islands
A hundred years ago, there were many blue parrots on the Lorazul islands. The inhabitants worshipped them and built temples to them. These birds are now endangered and it is forbidden to catch them. Last year, you could sometimes see some on Kuku, a remote desert island.

The message:
Mr Robón, Find me a pair of blue parrots for my collection. Your fee: 3 million pesetas.

- *¡Eh! Las islas Lorazul... Mi bisabuelo iba a menudo allí para estudiar las plantas.* Hey! The Lorazul islands... My great-grandfather often went there to study the plants.
- *Era botánico...* He was a botanist...
- *Y el hombre calvo estaba en esas islas para robar loros.* And the bald man was on those islands to steal some parrots.
- *Venid, os quiero enseñar una cosa en casa.* Come on, I want to show you something at home.

New words

el año	year	capturar	to catch
el loro	parrot	se puede	it is possible to, one, you can
el habitante	inhabitant		
el templo	temple	encontrar (ue)	to find
la pareja	couple, pair	estudiar	to study
la colección	collection		
la remuneración	fee, payment	interesante	interesting
la peseta	peseta (Spanish money)	hace	ago
		mucho(a)	a lot of, lots of, many
la planta	plant		
el botánico	botanist	en extinción	endangered
la desaparición	disappearance	prohibido(a)	forbidden
la temporada de lluvias	rainy season	pasado(a)	last, past
		alguno(a)	some
el gobernador	governor	remoto(a)	remote, far away
		una cosa	something
ver*2	to see	por desgracia	unfortunately, sadly
parecer*2	to look, to seem, to appear		
		muerto(a)3	dead
adorar	to worship	en el momento de	at the time of
construir*	to build	peligroso(a)	dangerous

Sancho Salchicha's disappearance

Back at home, María shows her friends an old letter addressed to her grandfather, Santiago. To find out what it says, read it and translate it into English.

Villaloros

Señor:

Por desgracia, probablemente su padre está muerto. Conocía bien nuestras islas, pero en el momento de su desaparición buscaba plantas en unas islas peligrosas y muy remotas. Estaba con dos amigos botánicos. Tenían un buen barco, pero era la temporada de lluvias.

Pedro Peperoni
Gobernador de las islas

---

2 *Ver* and *parecer* are only irregular in the *yo* form of the present tense: *yo veo* (I see) and *yo parezco* (I look/seem/appear).
3 This is always used with *estar* (to be), not *ser* (to be).

The preterite

Spanish uses the preterite tense to talk about once-only events that happened in the past (such as "I saw Rob yesterday"), as opposed to events that were happening or used to happen regularly. For example, in "I was reading when I heard the alarm. I called the police . . . ", the first verb (was reading) would be in the imperfect, and the others (heard, called) in the preterite.

Irregular verbs

Most verbs that are irregular in the present tense also have an irregular preterite.[1] Four useful ones are shown below.

Hacer (to do/make – preterite)

hice	I did/made
hiciste	you did/made
hizo	he/she/it/you did/made
hicimos	we did/made
hicisteis	you did/made
hicieron	they/you did/made

Ser (to be) and ir (to go)

Ser[2] and ir share the same preterite, shown here:

fui	I was/went
fuiste	you were/went
fue	he/she/it/you were/went
fuimos	we were/went
fuisteis	you were/went
fueron	they/you were/went

Dar (to give – preterite)

di	I gave
diste	you gave
dio	he/she/it/you gave
dimos	we gave
disteis	you gave
dieron	they/you gave

How to form the preterite

Usually, to form the preterite, you add one set of endings to the stem of "ar" verbs and a different set to the stem of "er" and "ir" verbs. "Ar" verb endings are: -é, -aste, -ó, -amos, -asteis and -aron. "Er" and "ir" verb endings are: -í, -iste, -ió, -imos, -isteis and -ieron.

La comida está casi preparada.

¿Compraste pan?

¡On no, lo siento, me olvidé!

No importa.

Hay que esperar a papá. Fue a una reunión que se termina a las dos.

¿Tienes la agenda?

¡María, las bicicletas! Está lloviendo . . .

No, la dejé en mi tienda de campaña. Esperad aquí.

No te preocupes, las metimos dentro.

New words

el pan	bread	olvidarse	to forget	lo siento	I'm sorry
la reunión	meeting	esperar (a)	to wait (for), to hope, to expect	no importa	it doesn't matter
la entrada	entrance			papá	Dad, Daddy
la cueva	cave	llover (ue)	to rain	dentro	inside
el cofre	chest	preocuparse	to worry	cómo	how
la llave	key	meter	to put in/inside	roñoso(a)	rusty
el dueño	owner, landlord	dejar	to leave (behind)	largo(a)	long
la caja fuerte	safe	lograr	to manage	como	as
la recompensa	reward	llegar	to arrive, to reach, to get		
comprar	to buy	ir de compras	to go shopping		

1 You will find out more about verbs with an irregular preterite on page 36, where the preterite of stem-changing verbs is also explained. 2 Remember that Spanish has two verbs for "to be", ser and estar. The preterite of estar is also irregular and is explained on page 36.

Speech bubble key

- *La comida está casi preparada.* Lunch is nearly ready.
- *¿Compraste pan?* Did you buy any bread?
- *¡Oh no, lo siento, me olvidé!* Oh no, sorry, I forgot!
- *No importa.* It doesn't matter.
- *Hay que esperar a papá. Fue a una reunión que se termina a las dos.* We have to wait for Dad. He went to a meeting which ends at two.
- *¡María, las bicicletas Está lloviendo . . .* María, the bicycles! It's raining . . .
- *No te preocupes, las metimos dentro.* Don't worry, we put them inside.
- *¿Tienes la agenda?* Have you got the diary?
- *No, la dejé en mi tienda de campaña. Esperad aquí.* No, I left it in my tent. Wait here.
- *Oh . . . Aquí explica cómo encontró la carta de Sancho Salchicha.* Oh . . . Here he explains how he found Sancho Salchicha's letter.
- *Buscaba loros azules.* He was looking for blue parrots.
- *Logró llegar a la isla Kuku.* He managed to get to Kuku island.
- *A la entrada de una cueva, vio[3] un cofre viejo y roñoso.* At the entrance to a cave, he saw a rusty old chest.
- *Dentro encontró una carta que hablaba de un tesoro.* Inside he found a letter that talked of treasure.
- *Sí, la carta que robó . . .* Yes, the letter that he stole . .
- *¡Venid a la mesa!, papá está aquí.* Come and eat, here's Dad!
- *Lo siento, pero la reunión fue muy larga.* Sorry, but the meeting was very long.

Telling a story

Try telling this story using all the right tenses. You will have to put two verbs into the imperfect and six into the preterite.

Dos amigos, Miguel y Paco (ir) de compras, (buscar[5]) unos vaqueros. En una tienda (encontrar) unas llaves en el bolsillo de unos vaqueros. Se las (dar) al dueño de la tienda. "¡Las llaves de mi caja fuerte! ¡Gracias! Las (perder) ayer. Las (buscar[5]) por todas partes, pero no las (encontrar)." Como recompensa, les (dar) los vaqueros.

3 Notice that *ver* (to see), which is irregular in the present tense, is regular in the preterite. A few verbs are like this – see page 36. **4** Careful: the "c" in *buscar* changes to "qu" in front of an "e".

35

Irregular preterites

As explained on page 34, most verbs that are irregular in the present tense are also irregular in the preterite.[1] A few, such as *hacer*, *ser*, *ir* and *dar* (see page 34), have very irregular preterites which you have to learn one by one. However, most verbs with an irregular preterite simply have a special, preterite stem (that you have to learn), to which you add the following set of endings: -*e*, -*iste*, -*o*, -*imos*, -*isteis* and -*ieron* (-*eron* for the three verbs *conducir*, *decir* and *traer*).

Irregular preterite stems

The most useful verbs that take the preterite endings -*e*, -*iste*, -*o*, etc. are shown here with their preterite stem. (Notice that the list includes *andar*, which is regular in the present tense, and two stem-changing verbs, *poder* and *querer*.)

andar (to walk), preterite stem: *anduv-*
estar (to be): *estuv-*
poder (to be allowed to, can, may, might): *pud-*
poner (to put): *pus-*
querer (to want): *quis-*

saber (to know): *sup-*
tener (to have): *tuv-*
venir (to come): *vin-*

conducir (to drive): *conduj-*
decir (to say): *dij-*
traer (to bring): *traj-*

Speech bubble key

- *Tenemos que ir a la granja Tres Robles . . .* We must go to Tres Robles Farm . . .
- *para encontrar al señor Robón y la pista del colegio.* to find Mr Robón and the clue from the school.
- *¿Café, señor Robón?* Some coffee, Mr Robón?
- *Gracias . . . Em, quería hacerles una pregunta . . .* Thank you . . . Er, I wanted to ask you . . .
- *Esta mañana estuve en Villatorres.* I was in Villatorres this morning.
- *Vi el castillo y las dos torres . . .* I saw the castle and the two towers . . .
- *pero no pude encontrar la torre en ruinas.* but I couldn't find the ruined tower.
- *¿Por qué quiere verla? Solamente hay algunas piedras viejas.* Why do you want to see it? There's only a few old stones.
- *Er . . . Me gustan las ruinas.* Er . . . I like ruins.
- *Bien, ¿fue al parque?* Well, did you go to the park?

---

36 1 Exceptions are: *conocer* (to know), *salir* (to go out) and *ver* (to see). These are irregular in the present tense but not in the preterite.

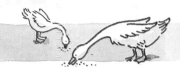

The preterite of stem-changing verbs

In the preterite, "ar" stem-changing verbs and most "er" stem-changing verbs have no stem change and behave just like regular "ar" and "er" verbs (see page 34). *Poder* and *querer* are exceptions. They have irregular preterites (see opposite page).

"Ir" stem-changing verbs do have a stem change in the preterite. This only affects the *él/ella/Ud.* and *ellos(as)/Uds.* forms, and involves an "e" changing to an "i" and an "o" changing to a "u". These verbs take the same preterite endings as regular "ir" verbs (see page 34), for example *pedí* (I ordered/asked for), *pidió* (he/she ordered).

(see page 34)

Sí, Yolanda tuvo un ternero precioso ayer por la noche.

Me acosté a las dos de la madrugada.

Sí, están bien.

El veterinario vino a verlos esta mañana.

. . . Sí, la torre en ruinas está al lado del río.

La próxima pista debe estar en la torre vieja.

¿Ah sí? Muy interesante . . .

New words

la piedra	stone
la ruina	ruin
el parque	park
el ternero	calf
la madrugada	morning (midnight to 5 or 6 a.m.), the small hours
el veterinario	vet
conducir*	to drive
encontrar (ue)	to find
hacer una pregunta	to ask a question
bajar	to go down
esta mañana	this morning
en ruinas	ruined, in ruins
solamente	only
algunos(as)	a few, some
precioso(a)	lovely, beautiful

Say it in Spanish

Put these sentences into Spanish. All the verbs must go into the preterite.

Señor Robón looked for the ruined tower, but he didn't find it.
Carmen, Fede and María went to the farm.
They found Señor Robón.
He didn't see them.
Carmen and María hid under the window.
The woman served coffee.

●*Sí, conduje hasta allí, pero no vi nada.* Yes, I drove over there, but I didn't see anything.
●*¡Ah! Usted no bajó hasta el río.* Ah! You didn't go down to the river.
●*Sí, Yolanda tuvo un ternero precioso ayer por la noche.* Yes, Yolanda had a lovely calf last night.
●*Me acosté a las dos de la madrugada.* I went to bed at two o'clock in the morning.
●*Sí, están bien.* Yes, they're well.
●*El veterinario vino a verlos esta mañana.* The vet came to see them this morning.
●. . . *Sí, la torre en ruinas está al lado del río.* . . . Yes, the ruined tower is by the river.
●*¿Ah sí? Muy interesante . . .* Ah yes? Very interesting . . .
●*La próxima pista debe estar en la torre vieja.* The next clue must be at the old tower.

The perfect tense

The English perfect tense is made from "to have" + a form of the verb called the past participle, e.g. "I have eaten". Spanish also has a perfect tense that it uses in the same way. To form it, you use the present tense of *haber*, a special verb for "to have"[1] (*he, has, ha,* *hemos, habéis, han*) + the past participle of the verb you want. To form the past participle, you normally add *-ado* to the stem of "ar" verbs and *-ido* to that of "er" and "ir" verbs. For example, *He comido* (I have eaten), *María ha vivido aquí* (María has lived here).

Irregular past participles

A few regular, irregular and stem-changing verbs have irregular past participles that you must learn, for example:[2]

abierto (from *abrir* – to open)
hecho (from *hacer** – to do, to make)
puesto (from *poner** – to put)
visto (from *ver** – to see)
vuelto (from *volver (ue)* – to return, to come back)

Entonces, ha descifrado la pista del colegio . . .

Pero todavía no la ha encontrado.

y ahora quiere ir a la torre en ruinas.

Entonces, tenemos que ir allí ahora mismo, antes que él.

Hemos vuelto porque necesitamos las bicis.

Hola señora, ¿puede arreglar esta oreja que está rota?

"Mine", "yours", "his", "hers", etc.

For "mine", "yours", etc, Spanish has a special set of words (see right). These change to match the noun they are replacing. For example, talking about a bag (*un bolso*), you say *El mío es azul* (Mine is blue), but for a suitcase (*una maleta*), you say *La mía es azul.*

With *ser*, you drop the words *el, la, los* and *las*: *Es mío/mía* (It's mine). Also, with *ser*, to say that something is "his", "hers" and "yours" (polite), you can either use *suyo* or *de* + *él/ella/Ud./Uds.* For example, you can say either *Es suyo* or *Es de él*[3] (It's his).

(m)	(f)	(m pl)	(f pl)	
el mío	la mía	los míos	las mías	mine
el tuyo	la tuya	los tuyos	las tuyas	yours
el suyo	la suya	los suyos	las suyas	his/hers/its/yours
el nuestro	la nuestra	los nuestros	las nuestras	ours
el vuestro	la vuestra	los vuestros	las vuestras	yours
el suyo	la suya	los suyos	las suyas	theirs/yours

Realmente nunca he explorado la torre porque hay una valla.

¿De quién es esta gorra?

¡Es de él!

1 As opposed to the usual verb for "to have", *tener* (see page 8). **2** For a more complete list, see page 53. **3** This is the same as when you say things like *Es de Fede* (It's Fede's), as explained on page 12.

New words

la bici	bike	conservar	to keep, to preserve
la oreja	ear	destruir	to destroy
la valla	fence	vengarse	to get your revenge
la gorra	cap	ganar	to win, to earn
el monumento	monument	expulsar	to expel
el pirata	pirate	desaparecer	to disappear
la batalla	battle		
el fuerte	fort	todavía no	not yet
el país	country	antes que	before
		realmente	really
descifrar	to decipher, to figure out	verdad	true
		nada	nothing
necesitar	to need	por todas partes	everywhere
explorar	to explore	sagrado(a)	sacred
examinar	to examine	último(a)	last

The writing on the tower

Sancho Salchicha put his sign on an old plaque. This is what Fede, Carmen and María see when they clear away the ivy. It gives them a good idea of where to go next. Translate it and see what you think.

Hemos conservado esta torre en ruinas porque es un monumento sagrado para los habitantes de Villatorres.

Los piratas de la Isla de los Piratas la destruyeron hace tres años, pero ahora nosotros nos hemos vengado. Hemos ganado nuestra última batalla contra ellos, los hemos expulsado de su fuerte en la isla y han desaparecido de nuestro país.

Speech bubble key

● *Entonces, ha descifrado la pista del colegio . . .* So, he's figured out the clue from the school . . .

● *y ahora quiere ir a la torre en ruinas.* and now he wants to go to the ruined tower.

● *Pero todavía no la ha encontrado.* But he hasn't found it yet

● *Entonces, tenemos que ir allí ahora mismo, antes que él.* So we must go there right away, before him.

● *Hemos vuelto porque necesitamos las bicis.* We've come back because we need the bikes.

● *Hola señora, ¿puede arreglar esta oreja que está rota?* Hello. Can you mend this broken ear?

● *Realmente nunca he explorado la torre porque hay una valla.* I've never really explored the tower because there's a fence.

● *¿De quién es esta gorra?* Whose cap is this?

● *¡Es de él!* It's his!

● *No, él tiene la suya.* No, it's not, he's got his.

● *Mira, tú no tienes la tuya.* Look, you haven't got yours.

● *Oh, es verdad . . .* Oh, that's true . . .

● *¡Nada! He buscado por todas partes y examinado todas las piedras.* Nothing! I've looked everywhere and examined each stone.

● *¡Eh, he encontrado algo aquí!* Hey, I've found something here!

● *¡Mirad! . . . ¡Es la señal de Sancho Salchicha!* Look! . . . It's Sancho Salchicha's sign!

The future tense

Like English, Spanish has a future tense for talking about events in the future. This is usually used where English uses its future tense (We will/We'll walk).

How to form the future tense

The Spanish future tense is easy to form. For most verbs, you take the infinitive and add these future tense endings: *-e, -ás, -á, -emos, -éis, -án* (see the future tense of *andar* (to walk), below left. Stem-changing verbs (except for *querer* and *poder*) do not have a stem change and form the future in the same way. *Querer, poder* and a few irregular verbs do not use the infinitive to form the future, but have their own future stem instead (see box below). To form the future, you just add the future endings to the special stem.

Andar (future tense)

andaré	I will walk
andarás	you will walk
andará	he/she/it will walk
andaremos	we will walk
andaréis	you will walk
andarán	they/you will walk

Future stems to learn

decir (to say), future stem: *dir-*
hacer (to do, to make): *har-*
poder (to be able to, can): *podr-*
poner (to put): *pondr-*
querer (to want): *querr-*
saber (to know): *sabr-*

salir (to go out): *saldr-*
tener (to have): *tendr-*
venir (to come): *vendr-*

Note: the future of *hay* (there is/are) is *habrá* (there will be).

New words

la travesía	crossing
la noche	night
la hoja	leaf, sheet (of paper)
el rastro	trail
la nota	note
la dirección	direction, address
el sitio	place
la tierra	earth, soil, ground
la trampa	trap
la misión	task
el barrote	bar (on window)
el panel	panel
la madera	wood
la joya	jewel
la fortuna	fortune
ser de noche	to be night-time/dark
dejar	to leave (behind)
molestar	to disturb
ensuciar	to dirty
dibujar	to draw
caer en la trampa	to fall in the trap, to fall for it
durante	during
falso(a)	false
así	so, thus, in this way, that way
equivocado(a)	wrong
seguro que	definitely, most probably
por allí	that way, over/around there

Entonces, tenemos que ir a la Isla de los Piratas.

Será de noche y la travesía será peligrosa.

Hoy no, llegaremos demasiado tarde...

Pero el hombre encontrará la pista aquí y...

Bien, tenemos que esconder esta pista con hojas. ¡Ahí!

irá a la isla durante la noche.

También podemos dejar un rastro falso.

¡Buena idea! Así tomará la dirección equivocada...

y no nos molestará.

The false trail

This is María's note. She has used funny writing. To discover where she is sending the bald man, you will have to figure out how to read it. Then you can translate it into English

S.S. sóidA. ílla nátse
anutrof im y sayoj sim
sadoT. aredam ed selenap
noc derap anu
sárartnocne ortneD. ílla
rop sárartnE. setorrab
nis anatnev anu sáreV.
ojeiV otreuP ed aírasimoc
al a ri euq sárdneT. licífid
áreS. nóisim amitlú al
átse íuqA. odajed eh euq
satsip sal sadot
odartnocne sah arohA:
ojih odireuQ.

Speech bubble key

• *Entonces, tenemos que ir a la Isla de los Piratas.* So we must go to Pirates' Island.
• *Hoy no,[1] llegaremos demasiado tarde* . . . Not today. We'll get there too late . . .
• *Será de noche y la travesía será peligrosa.* It'll be night-time and the crossing will be dangerous.
• *Pero el hombre encontrará la pista aquí y* . . . But the man will find the clue here and . . .
• *irá a la isla durante la noche.* he'll go to the island during the night.
• *Bien, tenemos que esconder esta pista con hojas. ¡Ahí!* Well, we must hide this clue with leaves. There!
• *También podemos dejar un rastro falso.* We can also leave a false trail.
• *¡Buena idea! Así tomará la dirección equivocada* . . . Good idea! That way he'll go off in the wrong direction . . .
• *y no nos molestará.* and won't[2] disturb us.
• *Bien, debemos dejarle una nota.* Right, we must leave him a note.
• *Tengo una buena idea.* I've got a good idea.
• *¿Pero dónde la esconderemos?* But where shall[3] we hide it?
• *Fede y yo podemos buscar un buen sitio.* Fede and I can look for a good place.
• *Tendrás que ensuciar la nota con tierra.* You'll have to dirty the note with some soil.
• *Sí, . . . no te preocupes, será perfecto.* Yes, . . . don't worry, it'll be perfect.
• *Podemos esconderla aquí y dibujar su señal.* We can hide it here and draw his sign.
• *¡Qué buena idea! Seguro que caerá en la trampa.* That's a great idea! He's bound to (He'll definitely) fall for it.

---

1 Here, *no* comes after *hoy* for greater emphasis. 2 Note that "will not" turns into "won't". 3 "Shall" can be used in English instead of "will" in the "I" and "we" forms, especially in questions.

More about the future

Apart from the future tense, Spanish has another way of talking about the future. You can use the present tense of *ir* (to go – see page 22) + *a* + the infinitive of the verb you need.

This works exactly like the English "going to" future,

for example *Voy a abrir la puerta* (I'm going to open the door).[1] Just as in English, the "going to" method often replaces the future tense in everyday Spanish. As a general rule, use it whenever English might, but bear in mind that it is even more common in Spanish, especially for events that are just about to happen.

Vamos a cerrar . . .

Muy bien, voy a ordenar las cosas . . .

y después me voy.

Bien, buenas noches.

¡Eh! Éste es el hombre que los chicos me enseñaron . . .

Número 7454
Dirección:
Calle Lavapiés nº 48
Madrid 28050

Sí, es el mismo hombre.

¡Hola! ¿Madrid? Quisiera saber los detalles del número 7454.

Bien, voy a buscarlos y después se los enviaré por fax.

Muy bien, gracias.

"This (one)", "that (one)"

The Spanish for "this (one)" is *éste* [m] or *ésta* [f]. "These (ones)" is *éstos* [m pl] or *éstas* [f pl]. For "that (one)/those (ones)", Spanish either uses *ése* [m], *ésa* [f], *ésos* [m pl] and *ésas* [f pl], or, for things which are further away (i.e. "over there"), *aquél* [m],

aquélla [f], *aquéllos* [m pl] and *aquéllas* [f pl].

Three extra words, *esto* (this [one]), *eso* and *aquello* (that [one]), are used for things you don't know the gender of, for example *¿Qué es eso?* (What's that?).

The present used for the future

English can use a present tense to talk about a future event, especially with a time word, for example "I leave/I'm leaving tomorrow morning". Spanish can do the same, though only with the present (not the present progressive): *Salgo mañana por la mañana* (I'm leaving tomorrow morning).

¡Ah es ésta! Todas ésas tienen barrotes.

Bien, no será muy difícil.

Podré romper la ventana.

Primero, voy a cenar y volveré después. Será muy de noche.

42 1 Note that although in English you can also use "will go and" (I'll go and open the door), you cannot do this in Spanish.

New words

el detalle	detail	*muy*	very, really
el número	number	*difícil*	difficult, hard
el robo	theft	*por fin*	at last
el tren	train	*después*	later, then
		X años	X years old
abrir	to open	*se busca*	wanted
ordenar	to tidy up	*primero*	first (of all)
*irse**	to go away, to be off	*contento(a)*	pleased, happy
enviar por fax	to fax, to send a fax	*alto*	stop
cenar	to have supper	*detenido(a)*	under arrest
volver (ue)	to come back	*cuándo*	when
ayudar a	to help		

Ah, por fin . . .

Número 7454
Ramón Robón
41 años

Se busca por robo
Recompensa

Bien, mañana iré a
la casa Salchicha.

Probablemente
los chicos podrán
ayudarme a
encontrarlo.

Estarán
contentos – hay
una recompensa.

¡Oh! ¿Qué es
eso?

¡Es él! Eh . . . ¡Alto!
Está usted detenido.

Talking about the future

Here are eight sentences in English for you to translate into Spanish:

Her train will arrive at three.

They're going to go out this evening.
What are you going to do? (Use the *tú* form of the verb.)
I'm going to go to Villatorres tomorrow.
Tomorrow we'll know when she's

going to come.
We'll look for him.
He'll see.
Will you come with me? (Use the *usted* form of the verb.)

Making comparisons

Comparisons are when you say things like "taller" or "the tallest". In English you either make them like this (with "-er" or "-est"), or, for longer words, with "more" or "the most" (more important, the most important). Comparisons are made with either adjectives or adverbs (with most adverbs, you only use "more", "the most"). For example, with an adjective, "She's taller/the tallest", and, with an adverb, "It goes more/the most often".

Comparisons with adjectives

In Spanish, to make comparisons with adjectives, you normally use the words *más* (to mean "-er" or "more") and *el/la/los/las más* (to mean "the -est" or "the most"). These go before the adjective and the adjective agrees with what it is describing. For example, with *alto(a)* (tall), you say *La mujer es más alta* (The woman is taller) or *Es la más alta* (She is the tallest).

"Than" and "as . . . as"

In comparisons, to say "than" as in "He's taller than his sister", Spanish uses *que*: *Es más alto que su hermana*.

To say "(just) as . . . as", for example "(just) as tall as", you use *tan . . . como*, so you say *Es tan alto como su hermana* (He's as tall as his sister).

Comparisons with adverbs

To say "-er/more" with adverbs, you do the same as with adjectives, except that there is no agreement – the adverb does not change. For example, with *lento* (slowly), you say *más lento* (more slowly).[1]

Common exceptions

Spanish has a few adjectives that do not use *más* for "-er/more" and *el más* for "-est/most", and a few adverbs that do not use *más*:

Adjectives With *bueno(a)* (good), you say *mejor, el/la/los/las mejor(es)* (better, the best). With *malo(a)* (bad), you say *peor, el/la/los/las peor(es)* (worse, the worst). With *grande* (big), you say *mayor, el/la/los/las mayor(es)* (bigger, the biggest).[2] With *pequeño(a)* (small), you say *menor, el/la/los/las menor(es)* (smaller, the smallest).[3]

Adverbs With *bien* (well), you say *mejor* (better). With *mal* (bad), you say *peor* (worse). With *poco* (few, little), you say *menos* (fewer/less).

Speech bubble key

●*¿Me puedes prestar tu toalla?* Can you lend me your towel?
●*¡Agh! Está tan mojada como la mía.* Yuk! It's as wet as mine.
●*¡Hola Rafa! ¿Tienes tu barca aquí?* Hi Rafa! Have you got your boat here?
●*Sí, está allí.* Yes, it's over there.

●*¿Nos la prestas? Queremos ir a la Isla de los Piratas.* Can you lend it to us? We want to go to Pirates' Island.
●*Sí, claro. Es la más pequeña.* Yes, of course. It's the smallest.
●*¡Cuidado! Uno de los remos es más corto que el otro.* Watch out, one of the oars is shorter than the other.

●*¡Eh! Estamos empezando a hacer círculos.* Hey! We're starting to go around in circles.
●*Sí, ¡Fede! No estás remando tan de prisa como yo.* Yes, Fede! You're not rowing as fast as me.
●*Tú tienes el mejor remo.* You've got the best oar.

1 The Spanish for "-est/the most" with adverbs is highly complicated and not often used. **2** You can also make comparisons with *grande* in the usual way (with *más* and *el/la/los/las más*) to mean "bigger, the biggest". *Mayor, el/la/los/las mayor(es)* can also mean "older, the oldest", when talking about people, despite the fact that the word for "old" is *viejo*. **3** You can also

New words

la toalla	towel	*hacer círculos*	to go around in circles	*mojado(a)*	wet
la barca	(rowing) boat			*corto(a)*	short
el remo	oar	*remar*	to row	*fuerte*	strong, loud(ly)
el calabozo	dungeon	*soler (ue)*	to be used to, to be in the habit of, to usually/ normally...	*raro(a)*	weird, strange, odd, unusual
el túnel	tunnel			*al final de*	at/to the end of
la barrera	gate, barrier			*¿cúal?*	which (one)?
prestar	to lend			*segundo(a)*	second

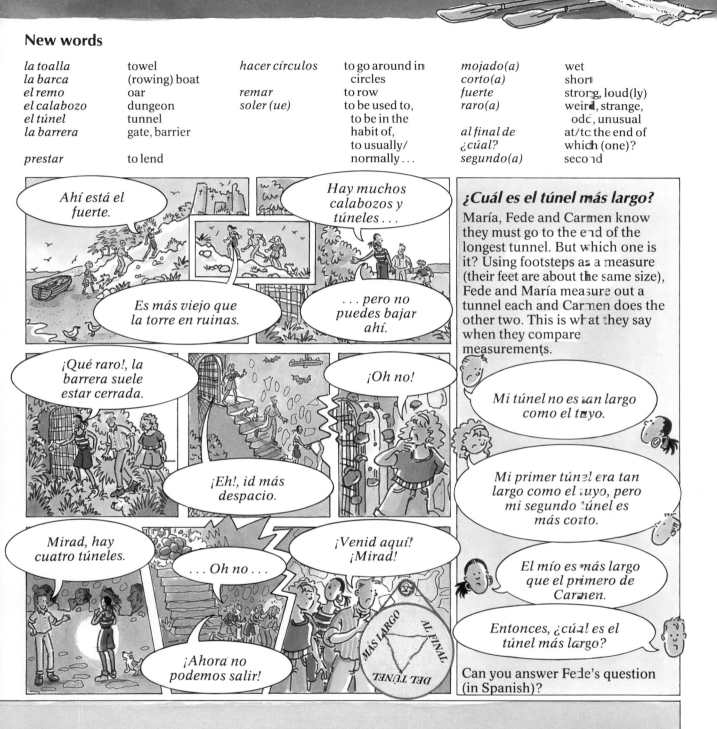

¿Cuál es el túnel más largo?

María, Fede and Carmen know they must go to the end of the longest tunnel. But which one is it? Using footsteps as a measure (their feet are about the same size), Fede and María measure out a tunnel each and Carmen does the other two. This is what they say when they compare measurements.

Can you answer Fede's question (in Spanish)?

- *No, soy más fuerte que tú.* No, I haven't, I'm stronger than you.
- *Ahí está el fuerte.* There's the fort.
- *Es más viejo que la torre en ruinas.* It's older than the ruined tower.
- *Hay muchos calabozos y túneles...* It's got lots of dungeons and tunnels...
- *... pero no puedes bajar ahí...* but you can't go down there.
- *¡Qué raro!, la barrera suele estar cerrada.* How odd, the gate's normally shut.
- *¡Eh!, id más despacio.* Hey, go more slowly.
- *¡Oh no!* Oh no!
- *Mirad, hay cuatro túneles.* Look, there are four tunnels.
- *... Oh no ...... Oh no ...*
- *¡Ahora no podemos salir!* We can't get out now!
- *Venid aquí! ¡Mirad!* Come here! Look at this!

make comparisons with *pequeño* in the usual way (with *más* and *el/la/los/las más*) to mean "smaller, the smallest". *Menor, el/la/los/las menor(es)* can also mean "younger, the youngest", when talking about people, despite the fact that the word for "young" is *joven*.

The conditional

In English, you make the conditional form of a verb with "would" (or just "'d"), for example "I would (I'd) ask her, but she's too busy". To make the conditional of most Spanish verbs, you add the "er" and "ir" verb imperfect tense endings (see page 32) to the verb's future stem. This means that the conditional of *andar* looks as shown on the right.

Si (if)

The word for "if" is *si*. Like "if", it is used with various tenses depending on what you are saying.

For anything that you are simply imagining, such as "If I had lots of money, I'd go to New York", you use *si* with the verb that follows it in a tense called the imperfect subjunctive and the "would" verb in the conditional. To form the subjunctive, you take the

Andar ("would" form)

andaría	I would/'d walk
andarías	you would walk
andaría	he/she/it/you would walk
andaríamos	we would walk
andaríais	you would walk
andarían	they/you would walk

ellos/ellas form of the preterite (see pages 34 and 36), drop "on" from the end, and add the endings *-a, -as, -a, -amos, -ais, -an*. This means that you say *Si tuviera mucho dinero, iría a Nueva York*.

Otherwise, you use *si* with the present and future tenses: *Si tengo suficiente dinero, iré contigo* (If I have enough money, I'll come with you).

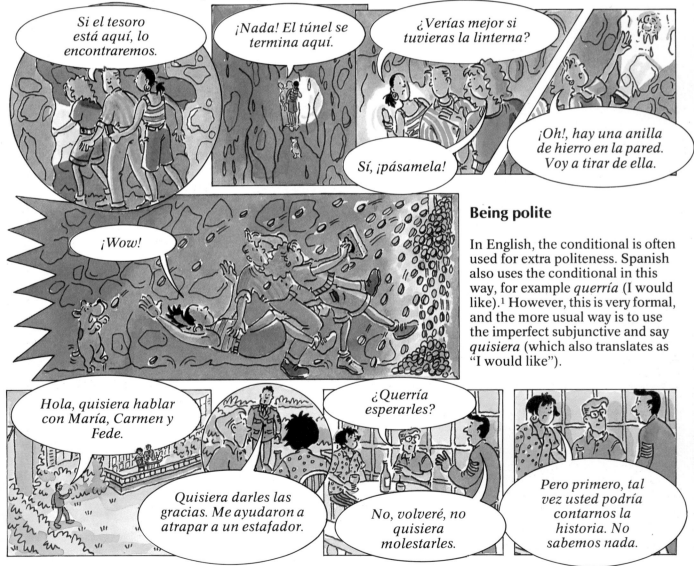

Si el tesoro está aquí, lo encontraremos.

¡Nada! El túnel se termina aquí.

¿Verías mejor si tuvieras la linterna?

Sí, ¡pásamela!

¡Oh!, hay una anilla de hierro en la pared. Voy a tirar de ella.

¡Wow!

Being polite

In English, the conditional is often used for extra politeness. Spanish also uses the conditional in this way, for example *querría* (I would like).[1] However, this is very formal, and the more usual way is to use the imperfect subjunctive and say *quisiera* (which also translates as "I would like").

Hola, quisiera hablar con María, Carmen y Fede.

Quisiera darles las gracias. Me ayudaron a atrapar a un estafador.

¿Querría esperarles?

No, volveré, no quisiera molestarles.

Pero primero, tal vez usted podría contarnos la historia. No sabemos nada.

46   1 Literally, *querría* means "I would want", but in English "I would like" is more natural.

New words

el dinero	money	dar las gracias	to thank
la anilla	ring	atrapar	to catch
el hierro	iron	contar (ue)	to tell, to count
la historia	story, history	mover	to move
el escalón	step	regalar	to treat (someone to), to give, to offer
la luz	light		
la roca	rock	gastar	to spend (money)
la entrada	entrance	reparar	to have mended, to fix
el par	pair		
el tejado	roof	Nueva York	New York
la tía	aunt	suficiente	enough
el oro	gold	seguramente	probably
		nuevo(a)	new
tirar de	to pull on, to give (something) a pull	Canadá	Canada

What if?

When the three get back to the Salchicha house, María asks her mother what she would do if she suddenly had lots of money. To complete Alicia's answers, you must put the verbs in brackets into the right form.

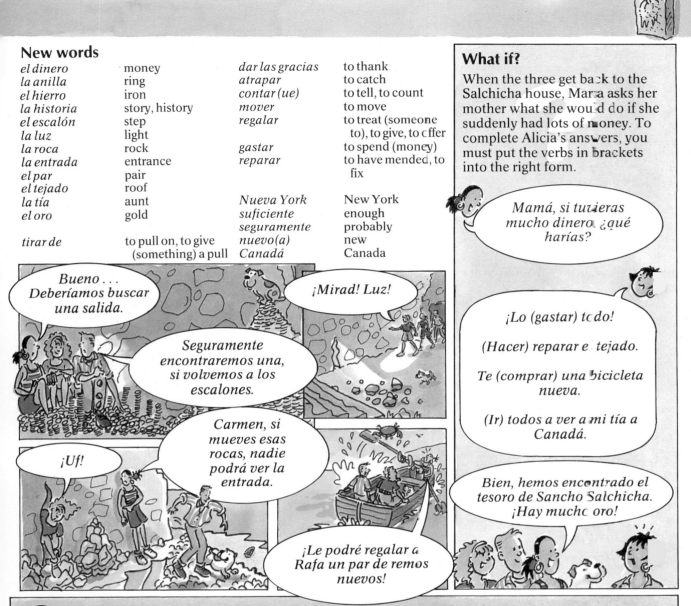

Mamá, si tuvieras mucho dinero, ¿qué harías?

¡Lo (gastar) todo!

(Hacer) reparar el tejado.

Te (comprar) una bicicleta nueva.

(Ir) todos a ver a mi tía a Canadá.

Bien, hemos encontrado el tesoro de Sancho Salchicha. ¡Hay mucho oro!

Bueno... Deberíamos buscar una salida.

¡Mirad! Luz!

Seguramente encontraremos una, si volvemos a los escalones.

Carmen, si mueves esas rocas, nadie podrá ver la entrada.

¡Uf!

¡Le podré regalar a Rafa un par de remos nuevos!

Speech bubble key

- *Si el tesoro está aquí, lo encontraremos.* If the treasure's here, we'll find it.
- *¡Nada! El túnel se termina aquí.* Nothing, the tunnel ends here.
- *¿Verías mejor si tuvieras la linterna?* Would you see better if you had the torch?
- *Sí, ¡pásamela!* Yes, pass it to me!
- *¡Oh!, hay una anilla de hierro en la pared. Voy a tirar de ella.* Oh, there's an iron ring in the wall. I'm going to give it a pull.
- *¡Wow!* Wow!
- *Hola, quisiera hablar con María, Carmen y Fede.* Hello, I'd like to talk to María, Carmen and Fede.
- *Quisiera darles las gracias. Me ayudaron a atrapar a un estafador.* I'd like to thank them. They helped me to catch a crook.
- *¿Querría esperarles?* Would you like to wait for them?
- *No, volveré, no quisiera molestarles.* No, I'll come back, I wouldn't want to disturb you.
- *Pero primero, tal vez usted podría contarnos la historia. No sabemos nada.* But first, you could[2] perhaps tell us the story. We don't know anything.
- *Bueno... Deberíamos buscar una salida.* Right... We should[3] look for a way out.
- *Seguramente encontraremos una, si volvemos a los escalones.* We will probably find one if we go back to the steps.
- *¡Mirad! Luz!* Look! Light!
- *¡Uf!* Phew!
- *Carmen, si mueves esas rocas, nadie podrá ver la entrada.* Carmen, if you move those rocks, nobody'll be able to see the entrance.
- *¡Le[4] podré regalar a Rafa un par de remos nuevos!* I'll be able to treat Rafa to (give Rafa) a new pair of oars!

2 Note: the conditional form of "can" is "could". 3 Note: the conditional form of "must, have to" is "should". 4 Notice the Spanish uses le ([to] him – see page 28) even though with "Rafa" in the sentence, "[to] him" is not needed as well. This is a frequent habit in Spanish that you will get used to.

A letter to read

Here is a letter with a newspaper cutting that María sent to Fede and Carmen after they went home to Madrid. There is a lot of Spanish for you to go through and make sense of. You can check how well you have done by looking at the English translations on page 57. There are also some useful words here for writing letters in Spanish.

Letter-writing tips

If the date is Tuesday, September 7th, you either write *martes, 7 de septiembre* (word for word, "Tuesday, 7 of September") or just *7 de septiembre* ("7 of September".[1] Days of the week and months are listed on page 58. For "Dear" at the start of a card or letter, you write *Querido* + a masculine name or *Querida* + a feminine one (*Queridos* or *Queridas* in the plural), and then you put a colon (:). To sign off, you can write *Con cariño* (literally, "With affection"), *Abrazos* (Hugs), *Besos* (Kisses) or *Muchos besos* (Lots of kisses). These are all the rough equivalent of "Love from" or "Love and kisses".

lunes, 2 de septiembre

Queridos Fede y Carmen:
Aquí está el artículo de la Voz de Villatorres que cuenta nuestra historia. ¡Es fenomenal! ¿Qué vais a hacer con vuestra parte de la recompensa? Con la mía, yo voy a comprar un radiocassette.
Si vuestra madre está de acuerdo, iré a vuestra casa durante las vacaciones de Navidad, así que ¡hasta pronto!, espero.

Muchos besos,
María

LA VOZ DE VILLATORRES
Viernes, 30 de agosto

El tesoro de la familia Salchicha

María Salchicha con sus amigos Fede y Carmen y su perro Guau Guau

Para María Salchicha y sus amigos Fede y Carmen éste ha sido un mes de agosto apasionante. Encontraron un tesoro y ayudaron a la policía a atrapar a un estafador.

Hace unos meses Robón estaba en una de las islas Lorazul. Allí buscaba unos loros en extinción que quería robar. Se encontró una carta del bisabuelo de María, Sancho. Era una carta vieja dirigida al abuelo de María, Santiago, y abandonada en un cofre viejo en la isla tras la muerte de Sancho. La carta fue la primera pista en una búsqueda del tesoro. Ésta le llevó a Robón a Villatorres, donde estúpidamente la perdió. Fede y Carmen, que venían a pasar unos

Ramón Robón, el ladrón de pájaros en extinción que quería robar el tesoro de la familia

días con su amiga María, la encontraron. Los tres adolescentes lograron encontrar el tesoro (oro) escondido en el viejo Fuerte de los Piratas, antes que el estafador, y ayudaron a la policía a atraparlo.

Los tres héroes también han recibido una recompensa de 300.000 pesetas de la policía. ¡Les felicitamos!

New words

el artículo	article	*encontrarse (ue)*	to find by chance, to come across	*durante*	during
la voz	voice			*Navidad*	Christmas
el radiocassette	radio-cassette player	*perder*	to lose	*así que*	then, so
el mes	month	*pasar*	to pass, to spend (time)	*hasta pronto*	see you soon
la muerte	death			*dirigido(a) a*	addressed to
el adolescente	teenager	*recibir*	to receive, to get	*abandonado(a)*	abandoned, left
el héroe	hero	*felicitar*	to congratulate	*estúpidamente*	stupidly
estar de acuerdo	to agree	*fenomenal*	brilliant		

1 Note that in dates, you just use the number on its own. The only exception is when you are talking about a date, you say *el primero* (the first), although you still write *1*.

Spanish grammar summary

This section brings together and summarizes the main areas of Spanish grammar introduced in this book. It includes lists and tables that are useful for learning from. Remember that basic grammar terms, such as "noun" and "verb", are explained on page 5.

Nouns and *el, la*

All Spanish nouns have a gender. They are either masculine or feminine.

In the singular (when you are talking about one thing, e.g. "bridge" rather than the plural "bridges"), the word for "the" is *el* before masculine nouns and *la* before feminine nouns.

Examples:
el puerto (the port)
el maletín (the briefcase)
la casa (the house)
la torre (the tower)

How to tell a noun's gender

Many Spanish nouns end in "o" and many end in "a". Most of those ending in "o" are masculine and most of those ending in "a" are feminine. There are a few exceptions to this, though, so you should always learn nouns with *el* and *la* before them.

Some of the most useful exceptions to know about are:
a) nouns that end in "a" but are masculine:
el día (day)
el mapa (map)
el problema (problem)
b) nouns that end in "o" but are feminine:
la radio (radio)
la foto (photo)

Other endings that tell you the noun's gender are "*ción*" and "*dad*". Most nouns with these endings are feminine, for example:
la estación (station)
la ciudad (town)

Nouns and *un, una*

The word for "a" (or "an") is *un* before masculine nouns and *una* before feminine ones, for example:

un puerto (a port)
un puente (a bridge)
una casa (a house)
una torre (a tower)

Plural nouns

With plural nouns, "the" changes to *los* and *las*. You use *los* with masculine plural nouns and *las* with feminine plural nouns.

Examples:
los puertos (the ports)
los maletines (the briefcases)
las casas (the houses)
las estaciones (the stations)

In the plural, most Spanish nouns that end in a vowel ("a", "e", "i", "o" or "u") add "s" and most of those that end in a consonant add "es" (see the examples above).

Exceptions you need to know are a few of the Spanish nouns that end in "s" and do not change in the plural, for example, *el lunes* (Monday), *los lunes* (Mondays). Useful nouns of this sort are all the days of the week that end in "s" (see page 58).

Stress marks and word endings

As explained in the pronunciation notes on page 5, in Spanish, for words ending in any consonant except "n" or "s", you normally stress the last syllable, or part of the word. For words that end in "n", "s" or a vowel, you stress the second-to-last syllable. For example, in *andar* (to walk), you stress the last part, "*dar*", and in *la casa* (house), you stress the first part, "*ca*".

However, Spanish has words that don't follow this pattern. These words are written with a stress mark (´) over the vowel in the syllable that you must stress, for example *la estación* (station). Bear in mind that you cannot really predict which words have a stress mark (and therefore an unusual stress pattern). You just have to learn them.

Quite often, when word endings change because of the way the word is being used, a stress mark is added to keep the stress in its original place. For example, you write *Pasa la linterna* (Pass the torch), but *Pásame la linterna* (Pass me the torch).

Conversely, a stress mark is sometimes dropped because the new ending now means the stress falls naturally in the right place, so no mark is needed. For example, *el maletín* (whose stress mark shows you must stress "*tín*" instead of "*le*") drops the stress mark in the plural, *los maletines*, as you would now naturally stress "*tin*".

Prepositions (*de* and *a*)

Spanish prepositions (words like "of", "to", "at", "with" and so on) are easy to use. The most useful ones are listed on page 22. However, when you use *de* (of, from, by) and *a* (to, at) in front of *el*, *de* + *el* contract and become *del* and *a* + *el* become *al*, for example:

Luis sale del cine (Luis is coming out of the cinema)
Voy al cine (I'm going to the cinema)

De is particularly useful because it is used for saying whose something is, for example:

Los vaqueros de Carmen (Carmen's jeans)
Son de María (They're María's)
La camiseta de la chica (The girl's T-shirt)
El jersey del chico (The boy's sweater)

In Spanish, the preposition *a* is always used after a verb if the verb's direct or indirect object is a person (or a pet). This is true whether you are using a person's name or a noun referring to them, for example:

Visito a mi amigo (I'm visiting my friend)
Visito a María (I'm visiting María)

Adjectives

In Spanish, adjectives normally come after the noun they are used with, for example:

blanco (white) – *un gato blanco* (a white cat)
marrón (brown) – *un perro marrón* (a brown dog)

To make comparisons using adjectives – to say, for example, "He is as tall as my sister" or "She is more important than Rob", you use *tan ... como* (as ... as) and *más ... que* (more ... than). For a detailed explanation of comparisons, see page 44

Agreement of adjectives

Spanish adjectives agree with the noun (or pronoun) they are used with. This means they normally have slightly different forms for the two genders and the plural.

In most cases, the masculine form ends in "o" and the feminine form ends in "a", for example *blanco* [m] and *blanca* [f] (white). The others, in the main, end in "e" or a consonant, and they stay the same in the masculine and the feminine, for example *verde* [m and f] (green) and *marrón* [m and f] (brown). There are few exceptions, e.g. *trabajador* [m], *trabajadora* [f] (hard-working).

In the word lists in this book, adjectives that have two forms are shown in their masculine form with their feminine ending in brackets, e.g. *blanco(a)* means the [m] form is *blanco* and the [f] form is *blanca*.

In the plural, adjectives that end in a vowel add "s" and those that end in a consonant add "es", for example:

los gatos blancos (the white cats)
las vacas blancas (the white cows)
los loros verdes (the green parrots)
las hojas verdes (the green leaves)
los perros marrones (the brown dogs)
las tortugas marrones (the brown turtles)

Adjectives that go before the noun

A few adjectives break the general rule and are always used before the noun. These include special adjectives meaning "this" and "that" and those meaning "my", "your", "his", "her", etc. (see page 50) as well as adjectives of quantity such as *mucho(a)* (a lot of, many) and *poco(a* (a few).

In addition, the following very common adjectives can be used either before or after the noun, without this affecting their meaning: *bueno(a)* (good), *malo(a)* (bad), *primero(a)* (first), *segundo(a)* (second), *tercero(a)* (third) and the adjectives for "fourth", "fifth", "sixth", etc.

When *bueno, malo, primero* and *tercero* are used in front of a masculine noun, though, their masculine forms change a little. They all drop "o" from the end, so you use *buen, mal, primer* and *tercer*.

Examples:
un libro bueno OR *un buen libro* (a good book)
un libro malo OR *un mal libro* (a bad book)
el primer piso OR *el piso primero* (the first floor)

The adjective *grande* (big, large) can also be used before or after the noun, and its masculine form changes to *gran* when it is used before a noun. In addition, though, when it is in front of a noun, its meaning changes to "great, grand, impressive". For example, *un edificio grande* means "a big building", but *un gran edificio* means "a great building".

"This" and "that"

The words "this" and "that" (and their plurals, "these" and "those"), when used with nouns as in "this dog", are adjectives. The Spanish words for them agree with the noun you are using them with. The table below shows you which word to use.

You will see that Spanish has two sets of words for "that, those". *Ese*, *esa*, etc. are used mostly when the person talking is referring to something that is closer to the person being spoken to. *Aquel*, *aquella*, etc. are used for things that are not particularly close to either person.

with masculine nouns	with feminine nouns	
este	*esta*	this
estos	*estas*	these
ese	*esa*	that
esos	*esas*	those
aquel	*aquella*	that (there)
aquellos	*aquellas*	those (there)

"This (one)" and "that (one)"

"This (one)" and "that (one)" (and the plurals "these (ones)" and "those (ones)"), as in "This one's got a bone" and "That's a tough problem", are pronouns, that is, they are used to replace or refer to a noun. The Spanish words for them agree with the noun they are referring to. The table below shows which word to use.

in place of masculine nouns	in place of feminine nouns	
éste	*ésta*	this (one)
éstos	*éstas*	these (ones)
ése	*ésa*	that (one)
ésos	*ésas*	those (ones)
aquél	*aquélla*	that (one) (there)
aquéllos	*aquéllas*	those (ones) (there)

Note that, except for the additional stress marks, these pronouns are identical to the adjectives for "this, these" and "that, those" (see the first table above), and that, as with the adjectives, there are two sets of words for "that, those". The pronouns and the adjectives sound the same. The pronouns have stress marks just to make them look

different, to save confusion in written Spanish.

Spanish has three extra pronouns, *esto* (this [one]), *eso* (that [one]) and *aquello* (that [one] [there]) which never change. They are used to refer to something unknown, where the pronoun does not refer to a specific noun so you don't know what gender to use, for example:

¿Qué es eso? (What's that?)
Esto es tonto. (That's stupid.)

"My", "your", "his", "her", etc.

The words "my", "your", "his", "her", etc. are a kind of adjective. In Spanish, they agree with the noun they are used with. The table below shows you which word to use. Notice that most of these words are the same in the masculine and feminine forms. Only *nuestro* (our) and *vuestro* (your) have a feminine form:

with a singular noun [m/f]	with a plural noun [m/f]	
mi	*mis*	my
tu	*tus*	your
su	*sus*	his/her/its/your (polite)
nuestro(a)	*nuestros(as)*	our
vuestro(a)	*vuestros(as)*	your
su	*sus*	their/your (polite)

For example, with *la maleta* (suitcase), you would say *tu maleta*, and in the plural, *tus maletas* (your suitcases). Using *nuestro*, though, you would say *nuestra maleta* (our suitcase), and in the plural, *nuestras maletas* (our suitcases).

As you can see, there are three sets of words for "your". You use *tu* and *tus* where you would use the word *tú* for "you", *su* and *sus* where you would use *usted* or *ustedes*, and you use *vuestro(a)* and *vuestros(as)* where you would say *vosotros* or *vosotras*. The next section (below and above right) explains the difference between *tú*, *usted*, *ustedes*, *vosotros* and *vosotras*, which all mean "you".

The Spanish for "mine", "yours", "his", etc. is explained on page 38.

"I", "you", "he", "she", etc. (*yo*, *tú*, *él*, *ella*, etc.)

The Spanish for "I" is *yo*. Note that, unlike "I", it only has a capital first letter when it is at the start of a sentence.

The Spanish for "you" is either *tú*, *usted*, *ustedes*, *vosotros* or *vosotras*, although getting the right word is less complicated than this list implies.

For "you", Spanish makes a distinction between familiar (casual and friendly) forms and polite forms, depending on the person you are talking to. In addition, it distinguishes between singular "you" (used for one person) and plural "you", and also sometimes between masculine and feminine.

The familiar forms are:
a) *tú* (singular, masculine AND feminine). You say *tú* to a friend;

b) *vosotros* (masculine plural) and *vosotras* (feminine plural). You say *vosotros* to male friends and *vosotras* to female friends. Use *vosotros* for a mixture of male and female.

The polite forms are:
a) *usted* (singular [m] and [f]). You say *usted* when talking to someone you don't know well or someone older than you;
b) *ustedes* (plural [m] and [f]). You say *ustedes* to people you don't know well or who are older than you.

Usted and *ustedes* are often written in short form: *Ud.* and *Uds.* (You may also see *Vd.* and *Vds.*)

When you are not sure which form to use, go for the polite one. If the person wants you to use the familiar form, they will tell you. (There is a special verb, *tutear*, which means "to say *tú*". You may hear *Puedes tutearme.* It means "You can say *tú* to me".) Usually, though, when a child or teenager talks to another child or teenager, *tú* is used, even at a first encounter.

The Spanish for "he" is *él* and the Spanish for "she" is *ella*.

You can find out about the Spanish for "it" on the page opposite.

The Spanish for "we" is *nosotros* in the masculine and *nosotras* in the feminine. This means boys and men say *nosotros* and girls and women say *nosotras*. A mixture of the two would use the masculine *nosotros*.

The Spanish for "they" is *ellos* in the masculine and *ellas* in the feminine. This means that if "they" refers to some men or boys, you say *ellos*, and if it refers to some women or girls, you say *ellas*. For a mixture, you say *ellos*.

When "they" refers to things (e.g. talking about books, "they're on the shelf"), you use the verb on its own (see the section above right about "it" and "they").

Dropping "I", "you", "he", "she", etc. with verbs

In Spanish, verbs change their endings according to who is doing the action. English usually has two verb forms, the "I/you/we/they" form and the "he/she" form, e.g. "I/you etc. walk" and "he/she walks". In Spanish, there are different verb forms for *yo*, *tú*, *nosotros* and *vosotros*, there is one form shared by *él*, *ella* and *usted*, and another one shared by *ellos*, *ellas* and *ustedes*. (See, for example, the present tense of *andar* (to walk) shown right.)

Because of this, Spanish often does not use the words for "I", "you", "he", and so on, as the verb ending makes clear who is doing the action. For instance, for "I walk", the most natural thing to say is just *ando*.

The only times when you use *yo*, *tú*, *él*, etc. are when you want to emphasize who is doing the action, as in "**I** washed the dishes", or when the verb alone is not clear. For example, because *él* and *ella* have the same verb form, you might say *él* or *ella* if, without this, it would not be clear who you were talking about.

The Spanish for "it" and "they" (referring to things)

Spanish does not use any word for "it" when "it" is the subject of a verb, as in "it arrives". Instead, you use the verb on its own, so for "it arrives", you just say *llega* (literally, "arrives"). You always use the *él/ella* form of the verb with "it".

For "they" referring to things rather than people, you do the same thing, but using the *ellos/ellas* form of the verb, for example *llegan* (they arrive).

When "it" is the direct object of a verb, as in "Steve showed it to his friends", Spanish uses *lo* (to refer to something masculine) and *la* (for something feminine). When "it" is an indirect object, as in "He gave it a final polish", the Spanish word is *le*.

In the plural, where English uses "them", the direct object words are *los* (masculine) and *las* (feminine), and the indirect object word is *les*. As you can see, like English, Spanish uses a different word from the subject words *ellos* and *ellas* (they).

For more about *lo*, *la*, *le*, *los*, *las* and *les*, see Personal pronouns on page 52.

Verbs

All Spanish verbs end in "ar", "er" or "ir" in the infinitive, or basic, form (which, in English, is the "to" form, as in "to talk").

Examples:
andar (to walk)
comer (to eat)
vivir (to live)

Verbs have various tenses to show when their action takes place. For example, you can say "I walk", "I walked" and "I'll walk" – these are three different tenses of the verb "to walk". The most useful tenses in Spanish are explained in this book.

The present tense

In the present tense, most Spanish verbs follow one of three regular patterns according to their infinitive ending. They either follow the "ar", "er" or "ir" pattern. Two groups of verbs do not work like this, though: stem-changing verbs and irregular verbs (see right).

To make the three regular kinds of present tense, you take the verb's stem (the infinitive form minus the "ar", "er" or "ir" ending) and you add present tense endings. For "ar" verbs, these endings are shown by the present of *andar*. For "er" verbs, they are shown by *comer*, and *vivir* shows the endings for "ir" verbs.

Andar (to walk) – present tense

yo ando	I walk (am walking)
tú andas	you walk
él/ella/Ud. anda	he/she walks, you walk
nosotros(as) andamos	we walk
vosotros(as) andáis	you walk
ellos(as)/Uds. andan	they/you walk

Comer (to eat) – present tense

yo como	I eat (am eating)
tú comes	you eat
él/ella/Ud. come	he/she eats, you eat
nosotros(as) comemos	we eat
vosotros(as) coméis	you eat
ellos(as)/Uds. comen	they/you eat

Vivir (to live) – present tense

yo vivo	I live (am living)
tú vives	you live
él/ella/Ud. vive	he/she lives, you live
nosotros(as) vivimos	we live
vosotros(as) vivís	you live
ellos(as)/Uds. viven	they/you live

Verbs – learning tip

Where English uses the words "I", "you", "he", etc. in front of a verb, Spanish often uses the verb alone, so for "I live", *vivo* is usually enough (see Dropping "I", "you", "he", "she", etc. with verbs, page 50).

Because of this, the different tenses are usually listed without *yo*, *tú*, *él*, etc, and it is much easier to learn them like this. Here, present tense verbs are shown with *yo*, *tú*, etc. so that you can get used to them, but it is easier just to learn the verb forms (e.g. *ando*, *andas*, *anda*, *andamos*, etc.).

The present tense – uses

As you can see from the present tense of *andar*, *comer* and *vivir*, the Spanish present tense is used for an action that is happening now or one that happens regularly. This means that *ando* can either mean "I walk" or "I am/I'm walking", *andas* can either mean "you walk" or "you are/you're walking", and so on. Spanish does have its own "am ...-ing" form (the present progressive), though, which it uses to stress that an action is actually going on. For more about this, see The present progressive on page 52.

As in English, the present is also sometimes used instead of the future tense for something that is going to happen. For example, *Llego el 3 de agosto* means, word-for-word, "I arrive on the 3rd of August" but can be translated as "I'll arrive on the 3rd of August" or "I'll be arriving on the 3rd of August".

The present tense – stem-changing verbs

Some verbs, called stem-changing verbs, follow the regular present tense patterns (as far as their endings are concerned), but have a change in their stem in all forms except the *nosotros* and *vosotros* forms. For example, with *pensar* (to think), you say *pienso* (I think).

A stem-changing verb either has an "e", an "o" or a "u" that changes. (There are only a very small number of verbs where a "u" changes.) The changes can be summed up like this:

"e" in the stem changes to "ie" or "i"
"o" changes to "ue":
"u" changes to "ue".

The "e", "o" or "u" that changes is always the last one in the stem, e.g. *despertar* (to wake up) gives you *despierto* (I wake up).

As an example, of a stem-changing verb, here is the present tense of *pensar*:

Pensar (to think) – present tense

yo pienso	I think (am thinking)
tú piensas	you think
él/ella/Ud. piensa	he/she thinks, you think
nosotros(as) pensamos	we think
vosotros(as) pensáis	you think
ellos/ellas/Uds. piensan	they think

Stem-changing verbs are usually shown in word lists with their stem change in brackets, so for example, *dormir (ue)* (to sleep) tells you it is a stem-changing verb and its stem "o" becomes "ue" (in all present tense forms except *nosotros* and *vosotros*).

The only way to know which verbs are stem-changing is to learn them, so don't just learn "*dormir* (to sleep)", learn "*dormir (ue)* (to sleep)".

The present tense – irregular verbs

A few verbs, called irregular verbs, don't follow the regular patterns shown by *andar*, *comer* and *vivir*. They have their own present tense patterns that you have to learn for each verb. They are often verbs that you use a lot, such as *tener* (to have) and *ser* and *estar* (to be). These and other very useful irregular verbs are shown on pages 54-55. Word lists in this book show irregular verbs with an asterisk (*).

A few irregular verbs are easy to learn, though, as they only have an irregular *yo* form and otherwise follow the "ar", "er" or "ir" pattern. The most useful ones are shown here, with their *yo* form:

conocer (to know [someone]) – *conozco*
dar (to give) – *doy*
decir (to say) – *digo*
estar (to be) – *estoy*
hacer (to do, to make) – *hago*
poner (to put) – *pongo*
saber (to know [how to/that]) – *sé*
salir (to go out) – *salgo*
ver (to see) – *veo*

Ser and estar (to be)

Spanish has two verbs for "to be", *ser* and *estar*. Both are irregular (their various forms are shown on pages 54-55). You have to learn to use the right verb for "to be".

Ser is used to say what a person or thing is (their job or purpose), what they are like (in essence, or always, rather than fleetingly), and where they are from. *Ser* is also used for telling the time. For example, *ser* is used in the following statements:

Soy un técnico (I am a mechanic)
Es una fotocopiadora (It is a photocopier)
Esa casa es bonita (That house is pretty)
María es de España (María is from Spain)
Es la una (It's one o'clock)

Estar is used for things that change or are only true for a short time. It is also always used for saying where people and things are. For example:

Estoy cansado (I'm tired)
La puerta está abierta (The door's open)
La casa Salchicha está cerca de Villatorres (The Salchicha house is near Villatorres)
Fede y Carmen están en el jardín (Fede and Carmen are in the garden)

The present progressive

English uses the present progressive tense (as in "I am walking") rather than the present tense ("I walk") for anything that is currently happening. For example, to explain why someone can't come out, you might say "She's doing her homework", and if you are lost, you might say "Excuse me, I'm looking for the campsite".

Spanish also has a present progressive tense, but it is used when you want to stress that the action is happening now. In the two examples above, Spanish would use the present progressive for the first one, but for the second one, the present tense can also be used.

The Spanish present progressive is made with the present tense of *estar* (see page 54) plus the "-ing" form of the verb you are using. For all verbs except those noted below, to make the "-ing" form, you add *-ando* to the stem of "ar" verbs and *-iendo* to the stem of "er" and "ir" verbs.

Examples:
Está hablando (He's speaking)
Estamos comiendo (We're eating)
Estoy abriendo la puerta (I'm opening the door)

The ending *-iendo* is sometimes replaced by *-yendo*. This is because in Spanish, you normally don't use "i" between two vowels. You replace it by "y". For example with *leer* (to read), the "-ing" form is *leyendo* (reading).

"Ir" stem-changing verbs have an irregular "-ing" form in that they have a stem change. If they have an "e" in the stem, it changes to "i", and if they have a stem "o", it changes to "u", for example:

pedir(i) (to ask, to order), *pidiendo* (asking, ordering);
dormir(ue) (to sleep), *durmiendo* (sleeping)

Ir (to go), *poder* (can, may, might) and *venir* (to come) also have irregular "-ing" forms (*yendo*, *pudiendo* and *viniendo*), though they are hardly ever used.

Personal pronouns

The words *yo*, *tú*, *usted*, *él*, *ella*, *nosotros*, *vosotros*, *ellos*, *ellas* and *ustedes* (I, you, he, she, we and they – see page 50) are called personal pronouns. These pronouns sometimes change when they are the object of a verb (rather than its subject), for example in English, "I" becomes "me" ("I like dogs" but "Rover likes me").

Spanish personal pronouns do the same, but in addition, there are sometimes slightly different words for the two kinds of object,

direct and indirect. (In "Rover likes her", "her" is a direct object; in "Rover gives her the bone" or "Rover gives the bone to her", "her" is an indirect object.) The table below shows you all the Spanish words:

subject	direct object
yo (I)	*me* (me)
tú (you)	*te* (you)
él (he)	*lo* (him, it)
ella (she)	*la* (her, it)
usted (you)	*lo/la* (you)
nosotros (we)	*nos* (us)
vosotros (you)	*os* (you)
ellos (they)	*los* (them)
ellas (they)	*las* (them)
ustedes (you)	*los/las* (you)

indirect object	
me ([to] me)	*nos* ([to] us)
te ([to] you)	*os* ([to] you)
le ([to] him/it)	*les* ([to] them)
le ([to] her/it)	*les* ([to] them)
le ([to] you)	*les* ([to] you)

In Spanish, the indirect object pronoun already means "to me/you/him", etc, so you do not translate "to" into Spanish as a separate word. In the table, "to" is bracketed because it is not always needed in English – you can say "He passes the book to me" or "He passes me the book".

"It" and "them"

Remember that Spanish does not use a word for "it" as subject – it uses the verb on its own (see page 51). When "it" is a direct object, you use *lo* to refer to a masculine noun and *la* to refer to a feminine one. For the plural direct object "them", you use *los* (masculine) and *las* (feminine). When "it" and "them" are indirect objects, the Spanish words are *le* and *les*.

Personal pronouns and word order

Spanish personal pronouns normally go before a verb, for example *Rover me da el hueso* (Rover gives me the bone).

You always put an indirect object pronoun before a direct object pronoun, for example *Me lo da* (He gives it to me).

If you use both an indirect and a direct object pronoun and they both begin with "l", the indirect object (either *le* or *les*) is replaced by *se*, for example *Se lo da* (He gives it to them).

When you use one or more object pronouns with a verb in the present progressive, the pronoun(s) can go before or after the verb. If you place them after, you attach them to the end of the "-ing" form, so you can either say *Lo estamos comiendo* OR *Estamos comiéndolo* (We're eating it).

Similarly, when you use object pronouns in a sentence that has two verbs, a main verb plus one in the infinitive, e.g. "I want to see her", you can place the pronoun(s) before the verbs or after the second (infinitive) one, in which case you attach it to the end of the verb, e.g. *La quiero ver* OR *Quiero verla* (I want to see her).

With a verb in the imperative (see page 53), object pronouns are attached to the end of the verb (*¡Cómela!* – Eat it!) unless the sentence is negative (*¡No la comas!* – Don't eat it!).

Mí, ti (me, you)

When you use a personal pronoun after a preposition, as in "The salad is for him", you use all the subject forms (see left) except for *yo* and *tú*. Instead of these, you use *mí* and *ti*, for example *Este jersey es para mí* (This sweater's for me).

To say "with me" and "with you" (in the *tú* form), *con* (with) merges with *mí* or *ti* and you add "go" on the end: *conmigo* (with me) and *contigo* (with you).

Verbs – the imperfect tense

In Spanish, you use the imperfect tense for talking about events that were in the process of happening at a particular point in the past – where English uses "was/were + (verb + -ing)", as in "I was cycling" or "We were watching TV".

Spanish also uses the imperfect for descriptions of things in the past, as in "It was funny", and for an event that happened often or regularly – where English can say "I often cycled", "I cycled to school each day" or "I used to cycle to school".

To form the imperfect tense, you take the verb's stem and add one of two sets of imperfect tense endings, depending on whether the verb's infinitive ends in "ar", "er" or "ir". For verbs ending in "ar", you add the endings *-aba, -abas, -aba, -ábamos, -abais, -aban* (see the imperfect tense of *andar* below). For verbs ending in "er" and "ir", the endings are *-ía, -ías, -ía, -íamos, -íais, ían* (see the imperfect of *comer* below).

The only Spanish verbs which don't form their imperfect tense like this are *ir* (to go), *ser* (to be) and *ver* (to see). Their imperfects are shown on page 55. Stem-changing verbs have no change in their stem in the imperfect.

Andar (to walk) – imperfect tense

andaba	I was walking/ walked (often)
andabas	you were walking
andaba	he/she/it was walking, you were walking
andábamos	we were walking
andabais	you were walking
andaban	they/you were walking

Comer (to eat) – imperfect tense

comía	I was eating/ate (often)
comías	you were eating
comía	he/she/it was eating, you were eating
comíamos	we were eating
comíais	you were eating
comían	they/you were eating

The preterite

Spanish uses the preterite to talk about once-only past events – events that happened once at the time you are talking about or in the story you are telling. For example, all the verbs here would be in the preterite in Spanish: "That morning he cycled to school. He skidded on a banana skin and ended up in the pond."

For most Spanish verbs (exceptions are shown below), to form the preterite you take the verb's stem and add one of two sets of preterite endings, depending on whether the verb's infinitive ends in "ar", "er" or "ir". For "ar" verbs, you add the endings -é, -aste, -ó, -amos, -asteis, -aron (see the preterite of *cantar* below). For verbs ending in "er" and "ir", the preterite endings are -í, -iste, -ió, -imos, -isteis, -ieron (see the preterite of *comer* below).

Cantar (to sing) – preterite

canté	I sang
cantaste	you sang
cantó	he/she/it/you sang
cantamos	we sang
cantasteis	you sang
cantaron	they/you sang

Comer (to eat) – preterite

comí	I ate
comiste	you ate
comió	he/she/it/you ate
comimos	we ate
comisteis	you ate
comieron	they/you ate

There are three kinds of verb that form the preterite differently:

1) "Ar" verbs whose infinitive ends in -*car*, -*gar* or -*zar* such as *buscar* (to look for), *pagar* (to pay) and *empezar* (to start, to begin). These verbs have a spelling change in the *yo* preterite form. Their *yo* forms end in -*qué*, -*gué* and -*cé* respectively, for example *busqué* (I looked for), *pagué* (I paid), *empecé* (I started).

2) "Ir" stem-changing verbs. These verbs take the same preterite endings as other "ir" verbs, but have a stem change in the *él/ella/Ud.* and *ellos/ellas/Uds.* forms. This change involves an "e" in the stem changing to "i" and an "o" in the stem changing to "u". For example, the preterite *yo* form of *pedir (i)* (to ask for, to order) is *pedí*, but the *él* and *ellos* forms are *pidió* and *pidieron*. With *dormir (ue)* (to sleep), the *yo* form is *dormí*, the *él* form is *durmió* and the *ellos* form is *durmieron*.

3) Verbs with an irregular preterite. There are two types:
a) a few verbs that have very irregular preterite forms; important ones to know are *dar* (to give), *hacer* (to do, to make), *ir* (to go) and *ser* (to be) – see pages 54 and 55;
b) a few verbs that have a special stem in the preterite and which add a special set of preterite endings unlike the preterite "ar" and "er"/"ir" endings. This special set of preterite endings is -e, -iste, -o, -imos, -isteis, -ieron. The most useful verbs in this category are, with their preterite stems in square brackets:

andar (to walk) [*anduv-*]
estar (to be) [*estuv-*]
poder (to be allowed to, can, may, might) [*pud-*]
poner (to put) [*pus-*]
querer (to want) [*quis-*]
saber (to know) [*sup-*]
tener (to have) [*tuv-*]
venir (to come) [*vin-*]

Three verbs also work in this way, but their *ellos(as)/Uds.* ending is -*eron*, not -*ieron*, These are:

conducir (to drive) [*conduj-*]
decir (to say) [*dij-*]
traer (to bring) [*traj-*]

The present perfect

In English, the present perfect is the tense you are using when you say for example, "I have eaten" and "she has made". It is made from "have/has" + a form of the verb called the past participle (e.g. "eaten" and "made").

Spanish also has a present perfect tense which it uses wherever English does. It is made from the present of *haber* + the past participle of the verb you are using.

Haber is a special verb meaning "to have" which is mostly used to form tenses (not to say "I have (got)", for which you use the irregular verb, *tener*). Its present tense is *he, has, ha, hemos, habéis, han*. To form the past participle, for most "ar" verbs you add -*ado* to the stem, and for most "er" and "ir" verbs, you add -*ido* (-*ído* if the stem ends in "a", "e" or "o").

Examples:
he andado (I have walked, I've walked)
ha comido (he/she has eaten, (s)he's eaten)
han vivido (they have lived, they've lived)
han caído (they have fallen, they've fallen)

A few verbs have an irregular past participle that you have to learn. The most important ones that you should know are, with their past participles in square brackets:

abrir (to open) [*abierto*]
decir* (to say) [*dicho*]
cubrir (to cover) [*cubierto*]
descubrir (to discover, to find out) [*descubierto*]
escribir (to write) [*escrito*]
hacer* (to do, to make) [*hecho*]
morir (ue) (to die) [*muerto*]
poner* (to put) [*puesto*]
resolver (ue) (to solve) [*resuelto*]
romper (to break) [*roto*]
ver* (to see, to watch) [*visto*]
volver (ue) (to return) [*vuelto*]

The future tense

The Spanish future tense is usually used where English uses its future tense – where, for example, English says "I will (or "I'll") write", as in "I'll write the letter tomorrow".

To form the future tense of nearly all Spanish verbs, you take the infinitive form and add the following endings: -é, -ás, -á, -emos, -éis, án. For example, see the future tense of *andar* below.

Andar (to walk) – future tense

andaré	I will walk
andarás	you will walk
andará	he/she/it/you will walk
andaremos	we will walk
andaréis	you will walk
andarán	they/you will walk

The only exceptions are a few verbs that have a special future tense stem. For these verbs, instead of adding the future endings to their infinitive, you add them to this special stem. These verbs are, with their future stems in square brackets:

decir (to say) [*dir-*]
hacer (to do, to make) [*har-*]
poder (can, may, might) [*podr-*]
poner (to put) [*pondr-*]
querer (to want) [*querr-*]
saber (to know) [*sabr-*]
salir (to go out) [*saldr-*]
tener (to have) [*tendr-*]
venir (to come) [*vendr-*]

The imperative

The imperative form of a verb is used when you want to give a command – where, in English, for example, you say "Come here!". You always give a command to someone, so the imperative is always in the "you" form. With its four words for "you", Spanish has four imperative forms. You use the informal *tú* and *vosotros* forms to friends, and the polite *usted* and *ustedes* forms to older people and people you don't know well (see page 50).

Imperative *tú* form:
For most verbs, this is the same as the *él/ella/Ud.* present tense form, for example *¡Anda!* (Walk!). However, many irregular verbs have an irregular *tú* form imperative – see pages 54-55.

Imperative *vosotros* form:
For all verbs, you make this by taking the verb's infinitive and replacing the final "r" by a "d", for example *¡Andad!* (Walk!).

Imperative *usted* form:
For most verbs, this is made by taking the present tense *yo* form, dropping the final "o" and adding -*e* to "ar" verbs and -*a* to "er" and "ir" verbs, for example *¡Ande!* (Walk!), *¡Coma!* (Eat!).

Imperative *ustedes* form:
For most verbs, you make this like the *usted* imperative form, but you add -*en* to "ar" verbs and -*an* to "er" and "ir" verbs, e.g. *¡Anden!* (Walk), *¡Coman!* (Eat!).

A few irregular verbs have irregular *Ud.* and *Uds.* imperative forms (see pages 54-55).

In addition, in the *usted* and *ustedes* forms, for verbs with an infinitive ending in "*car*", "*gar*" and "*zar*", you take the present tense *yo* form as explained above, but there is a spelling change (the same as in the preterite). "C" changes to "qu", "g" to "gu" and "z" to "c", so from *buscar* (to look for), you say *¡Busque..!*, *¡Busquen..!* (Look for..!), from *pagar* (to pay), you say *¡Pague!*, *¡Paguen!* (Pay!) and from *empezar (ie)* (to start), you say *¡Empiece!*, *¡Empiecen!* (Start!).

Remember that if you use object pronouns with an imperative verb, they are attached to the end of it (see page 52).

Imperatives with *no*

In English, to tell someone not to do something, you use "do not" (or "don't"), as in "Don't eat that!". In Spanish, you simply use the verb in the imperative with *no* (not) in front of it. However, with *no*, the *tú* and *vosotros* imperative forms are not made in the usual way. Instead, they are made as follows.

Imperative *tú* form with *no*:
To make this, you take the present tense *yo* form and drop the "o". To this, you add -*es*

for "ar" verbs and -*as* for "ar" and "er" verbs, for example *¡No andes!* (Don't walk!) and *¡No comas!* (Don't eat!).

Imperative *vosotros* form with *no*:
To make this, you take the present tense *yo* form and drop the "o". To this, you add -*éis* for "ar" verbs and -*áis* for "er" and "ir" verbs, for example *¡No habléis!* (Don't talk!) and *¡No comáis!* (Don't eat!).

When you use an imperative with *no*, any object pronoun goes between *no* and the verb, e.g. *¡No lo lea!* (Don't read it!).

Reflexive verbs

Reflexive verbs are verbs such as *levantarse* (to get up) whose infinitive form always ends with *se*. In the various tenses, they normally begin with the words *me* (myself), *te* (yourself), *se* (him-/her-/it-/yourself, oneself), *nos* (ourselves), *os* (yourselves), *se* (them-/yourselves). For example, here is the present tense of *levantarse*.

Levantarse (to get up) – present tense

me levanto	I get up
te levantas	you get up
se levanta	he/she/it gets up, you get up
nos levantamos	we get up
os levantáis	you get up
se levantan	they/you get up

Reflexive verbs can be regular, irregular or stem-changing and they form their various tenses accordingly, with the addition of the small reflexive word. Regular and stem-changing reflexive verbs follow the patterns shown by the part of their infinitive that precedes -*se*, that is, "ar", "er" or "ir".

For example, here are the *yo* forms of *levantarse* in the various tenses:

imperfect tense: *me levantaba* (I was getting up/got up [often])
preterite: *me levanté* (I got up)
present perfect: *me he levantado* (I have got up)
future tense: *me levantaré* (I will get up)

In the imperative, the small reflexive word is kept, but it goes on the end of the verb. In addition, in the *vosotros* form, the -*d* imperative ending is dropped. For example:

tú form: *¡Levántate!* (Get up!)
vosotros form: *¡Levantaos!* (Get up!)
usted form: *¡Levántase!* (Get up!)
ustedes form: *¡Levántense!* (Get up!)

For *irse* (to go away), the *vosotros* imperative form can be either *¡Idos!* or *¡Iros!* (Go away!).

Negatives

Negative sentences are those with "not" (or "n't") in them, for example "I am not tired" or "I have not (or "haven't") got the time". In English you also often have to use "do" or "can" to make a negative sentence (you say "I don't smoke", "I can't see", not "I smoke not", "I see not"). In Spanish the verb does not change like this.

The Spanish for "not" is *no* (which also means "no"), and it goes before the verb, for example:

Carmen no quiere ver (Carmen doesn't want to see)
No quiero ver (I don't want to see)

Object pronouns in a negative sentence go between *no* and the verb, for example *No la veo* (I don't see her).

Question and exclamation marks

In Spanish, you always put an upside-down exclamation or question mark at the start of any exclamation or question. You also put an exclamation or question mark on the end, like in English, for example:

¡Qué alto! (How tall he is!)
¿Qué hora es? (What's the time?)

Note that the upside-down marks can go in mid-sentence, where the exclamation or question actually begins, e.g. *Hola, ¿cómo estás?* (Hello, how are you?).

Making questions

Note that the upside-down marks can go in of two ways. You can simply add question marks at both ends of a sentence, for example, to turn *Tú vienes* (You are coming) into *¿Tú vienes?* (Are you coming?). In spoken Spanish, raising your voice at the end makes clear this is a question.

The other way to make a question is to put the subject after the verb (you also add question marks in the usual way), for example *¿Vienes tú?* (Are you coming?) and *¿Viene Juan a la fiesta?* (Is Juan coming to the party?).

Remember that Spanish often leaves out the subject personal pronouns, *yo* (I), *tú* (you), *él* (he) and so on, as in *¿Vienes?* (Are you coming?). This means that the two methods often amount to the same thing, and only the question marks or the tone indicate a question.

With question words such as *¿dónde?* (where? – see list of question words on page 16), put the question word at the start of the question. If you are using a subject, this must go after the verb, for example *¿Dónde está la casa Salchicha?* (Where is the Salchicha house?).

Irregular verbs

Irregular verbs are verbs that have an irregular present tense – that is, a present tense that differs from the standard present tense patterns (see page 51) and which you have to learn individually. In addition, irregular verbs often don't follow the regular patterns for other tenses.

Remember, though, that a few verbs which follow the standard present tense pattern do sometimes behave like irregular verbs in other tenses (for example, *andar*, which has an irregular preterite). These are dealt with where each tense is introduced (see pages 51-54).

Many of the most commonly used verbs in Spanish are irregular. The most useful ones are shown here in the tenses and forms you will need. For each one, the following tenses are shown:

1) the present tense

2) the present progressive (not shown for verbs that you would not use in this tense)
3) the preterite
4) the present perfect (the *yo* form only, as this is enough to show the irregular part, the past participle)
5) the future tense (the *yo* form only – enough to show the special future stem)
6) the imperative forms (listed in the order: *tú, vosotros, usted, ustedes*).

All Spanish verbs except *ir*, *ser* and *ver* form the imperfect in a regular way (see page 52), so the imperfect tense of these three verbs only is shown.

Conocer (to know)
present tense

conozco	I know
conoces	you know
conoce	he/she/it knows, you know
conocemos	we know
conocéis	you know
conocen	they/you know

preterite

conocí	I knew
conociste	you knew
conoció	he/she/it/you knew
conocimos	we knew
conocisteis	you knew
conocieron	they/you knew

present perfect: *he conocido* (I have known)

future tense: *conoceré* (I will know)

imperative: *conoce, conoced, conozca, conozcan* (know)

Dar (to give)
present tense

doy	I give (am giving)
das	you give
da	he/she/it gives, you give
damos	we give
dais	you give
dan	they give

present progressive: *estoy dando* (I'm giving)

preterite

di	I gave
diste	you gave
dio	he/she/it/you gave
dimos	we gave
disteis	you gave
dieron	they/you gave

present perfect: *he dado* (I have given)

future tense: *daré* (I will give)

imperative: *da, dad, dé, den* (give)

Decir (to say)
present tense

digo	I say (am saying)
dices	you say
dice	he/she/it says, you say
decimos	we say
decís	you say
dicen	they say

present progressive: *estoy diciendo* (I am saying)
preterite

dije	I said
dijiste	you said
dijo	he/she/it/you said
dijimos	we said
dijisteis	you said
dijeron	they/you said

present perfect: *he dicho* (I have said)
future tense: *diré* (I will say)
imperative: *di, decid, diga, digan* (say)

Estar (to be)
present tense

estoy	I am (am being)
estás	you are
está	he/she/it is, you are
estamos	we are
estáis	you are
están	they/you are

preterite

estuve	I was
estuviste	you were
estuvo	he/she/it was, you were
estuvimos	we were
estuvisteis	you were
estuvieron	they/you were

present perfect: *he estado* (I have been)

future tense: *estaré* (I will be)

imperative: *está, estad, esté, estén* (be)

Hacer (to do, to make)

present tense

hago	I do (am doing)
haces	you do
hace	he/she/it does, you do
hacemos	we do
hacéis	you do
hacen	they/you do

present progressive: *estoy haciendo* (I am doing)

preterite

hice	I did
hiciste	you did
hizo	he/she/it/you did
hicimos	we did
hicisteis	you did
hicieron	they/you did

present perfect: *he hecho* (I have done)

future tense: *haré* (I will do)

imperative: *haz, haced, haga, hagan* (do)

Ir (to go)

present tense

voy	I go (am going)
vas	you go
va	he/she/it goes, you go
vamos	we go
vais	you go
van	they/you go

imperfect

iba	I was going/went (often)
ibas	you were going
iba	he/she/it was going, you were going
íbamos	we were going
ibais	you were going
iban	they/you were going

preterite

fui	I went
fuiste	you went
fue	he/she/it/you went
fuimos	we went
fuisteis	you went
fueron	they/you went

present perfect: *he ido* (I have been)

future tense: *iré* (I will go)

imperative: *ve, id, vaya, vayan* (go)

Poder (to be allowed/able to, can, may, might)

present tense

puedo	I can
puedes	you can
puede	he/she/it/you can
podemos	we can
podéis	you can
pueden	they/you can

preterite

pude	I could
pudiste	you could
pudo	he/she/it/you could
pudimos	we could
pudisteis	you could
pudieron	they/you could

present perfect: *he podido* (I have been able to)

future tense: *podré* (I will be able to)

imperative: not used

Poner (to put)

present tense

pongo	I put (am putting)
pones	you put
pone	he/she/it puts, you put
ponemos	we put
ponéis	you put
ponen	they put

present progressive: *estoy poniendo* (I am putting)

preterite

puse	I put
pusiste	you put
puso	he/she/it/you put
pusimos	we put
pusisteis	you put
pusieron	they/you put

present perfect: *he puesto* (I have put)

future tense: *pondré* (I will put)

imperative: *pon, poned, ponga, pongan* (put)

Querer (to want)

present tense

quiero	I want (am wanting)
quieres	you want
quiere	he/she/it wants, you want
queremos	we want
queréis	you want
quieren	they/you want

present progressive: *estoy queriendo* (I am wanting)

preterite

quise	I wanted
quisiste	you wanted
quiso	he/she/it/you wanted
quisimos	we wanted
quisisteis	you wanted
quisieron	they/you wanted

present perfect: *he querido* (I have wanted)

future tense: *querré* (I will want)

imperative: *quiere, quered, quiera, quieran* (want)

Saber (to know)

present tense

sé	I know
sabes	you know
sabe	he/she/it knows, you know
sabemos	we know
sabéis	you know
saben	they/you know

preterite

supe	I knew
supiste	you knew
supo	he/she/it/you knew
supimos	we knew
supisteis	you knew
supieron	they/you knew

present perfect: *he sabido* (I have known)

future tense: *sabré* (I will know)

imperative: *sabe, sabed, sepa, sepan* (know)

Salir (to go out)

present tense

salgo	I go out (am going out)
sales	you go out
sale	he/she/it/you go out
salimos	we go out
salís	you go out
salen	they/you go out

present progressive: *estoy saliendo* (I am going out)

preterite

salí	I went out
saliste	you went out
salió	he/she/it/you went out
salimos	we went out
salisteis	you went out
salieron	they/you went out

present perfect: *he salido* (I have gone out)

future tense: *saldré* (I will go out)

imperative: *sal, salid, salga, salgan* (go out)

Ser (to be)

present tense

soy	I am (am being)
eres	you are
es	he/she/it is, you are
somos	we are
sois	you are
son	they/you are

present progressive: *estoy siendo* (I am being)

imperfect

era	I was/was being/used to be
eras	you were
era	he/she/it was, you were
éramos	we were
erais	you were
eran	they/you were

preterite

fui	I was
fuiste	you were
fue	he/she/it was you were
fuimos	we were
fuisteis	you were
fueron	they/you were

present perfect: *he sido* (I have been)

future tense: *seré* (I will be)

imperative: *sé, sed, sea, sean* (be)

Tener (to have, to have got)

present tense

tengo	I have (got)
tienes	you have (got)
tiene	he/she/it has (got), you have (got)
tenemos	we have (got)
tenéis	you have (got)
tienen	they/you have (got)

present progressive: *estoy teniendo* (I am having)

preterite

tuve	I had (got)
tuviste	you had (got)
tuvo	he/she/it/you had (got)
tuvimos	we had (got)
tuvisteis	you had (got)
tuvieron	they had (got)

present perfect: *he tenido* (I have had)

future tense: *tendré* (I will have)

imperative: *ten, tened, tenga, tengan* (have)

Venir (to come)

present tense

vengo	I come (am coming)
vienes	you come
viene	he/she/it comes, you come
venimos	we come
venís	you come
vienen	they come

present progressive: *estoy viniendo* (I am coming)

preterite

vine	I came
viniste	you came
vino	he/she/it/you came
vinimos	we came
vinisteis	you came
vinieron	they/you came

present perfect: *he venido* (I have come)

future tense: *vendré* (I will come)

imperative: *ven, venid, venga, vengan* (come)

Ver (to see)

present tense

veo	I see (am seeing)
ves	you see
ve	he/she/it sees, you see
vemos	we see
veis	you see
ven	they/you see

present progressive: *estoy viendo* (I am seeing)

imperfect tense

veía	I was seeing/saw (often)
veías	you were seeing
veía	he/she/it was seeing, you were seeing
veíamos	we were seeing
veíais	you were seeing
veían	they/you were seeing

preterite

vi	I saw
viste	you saw
vio	he/she/it/you saw
vimos	we saw
visteis	you saw
vieron	they/you saw

present perfect: *he visto* (I have seen)

future tense: *veré* (I will see)

imperative: *ve, ved, vea, vean* (see)

Answers to quizzes and puzzles

Page 7 Getting to the Salchicha house

un café
un pueblo
un lago
una granja
un puente

Page 9 What is their luggage like?

2 *Sus maletas son grises.*
3 *Su bolso es azul.*
4 *Su maleta es verde.*
5 *Su maletín es rojo.*
6 *Su mochila es amarilla.*

Page 11 The mysterious letter

Una isla desierta, 1893

Mi querido hijo Santiago:

*Soy un hombre viejo. Estoy **solo** en mi isla desierta y **mi** casa cerca de Villatorres está **vacía**. Tengo **un** secreto. Soy muy **rico**. Ahora mi tesoro es tu tesoro. Mi casa **oculta** la primera pista. En primer lugar tú **buscas** los dos **barcos**.*

Adiós   Sancho Salchicha

A desert island, 1893

My dear son Santiago,

I am an old man. I am alone on my desert island and my house near Villatores is empty. I have a secret. I am very rich. Now my treasure is your treasure. My house hides the first clue. First of all you're looking for the two ships.

Farewell,   Sancho Salchicha

Page 13 De quién es?

2 *Esta mesa es de los vecinos.*
3 *Esta chaqueta es del huésped.*
4 *Esta camisa es de Alicia.*
5 *Estos vaqueros son de Fede.*
6 *Estas herramientas son del constructor.*

Page 15 The way to the old church

Girad a la izquierda.
Cruzad el puente.

Tomad el segundo camino a la izquierda.
Girad a la derecha.

Page 17 Shopping quiz

¿Dónde está el supermercado?
Quisiera un helado. ¿Cuánto valen?
¿Qué sabores tiene?
Quiero un kilo de manzanas, por favor.
¿Puede llevar mi cesta?

What does the letter mean?

Sancho Salchicha es el bisabuelo de María OR *Es el bisabuelo de María.*
Los dos barcos son dos cuadros OR *Son dos cuadros.*
Deben visitar el estudio (de Alicia/de la madre de María).

Page 19 The first clue

No hay dados.
No hay una vela OR *No hay vela.*
No hay un sombrero de copa OR *No hay sombrero de copa.*
No hay un libro OR *No hay libro.*
No hay un pájaro OR *No hay pájaro.*

Carmen, Fede and María have to go to El Mago (The Magician Inn).

Page 21 Crossword puzzle

Across
 1 *prefiere*
 2 *sí*
 3 *hoy*
 7 *un*
 8 *té*
 10 *sopa*
 11 *helado*
 12 *los*

Down
 1 *pista*
 4 *cerramos*
 5 *vuelves*
 6 *fotos*
 9 *jugar*

Page 23 The clue from the inn

(La vaca está/Está) encima de la colina (OR en/sobre la colina).
(El perro está/Está) debajo del árbol (OR al lado del/junto al/cerca del árbol).

(El banco está/Está) enfrente de la fuente (OR delante de/cerca de/junto a/al lado de la fuente).
(La granja está/Está) al lado de la iglesia (OR junto a / cerca de la iglesia).

Carmen's sentence ends:

. . . al colegio.

Page 25 A postcard from Carmen

Los vecinos (de los padres de María) tienen una cabra.
Carmen y Fede duermen/Duermen en las tiendas de campaña (que están en el jardín).
Carmen se despierta/Se despierta a las seis.
Fede se despierta/Se despierta a las ocho.
Carmen y Fede se acuestan/Se acuestan a las nueve y media o a las diez.

Page 27 Mix and match

No podemos ir ahora porque estamos comiendo.
Me llevo la bicicleta para ir a Puerto Viejo.
Conocemos a la señora Pastilla porque trabaja en la farmacia.
¡Silencio! Tengo que pensar porque es muy difícil.
Va a Villatorres para hacer compras.
El técnico está aquí porque la máquina está rota.

Page 29 The postcard jigsaw

Ramón Robón
Calle Palencia 59
28040 Madrid

Querido Ramón:

Gracias por tu carta. Sí, Antonio y Ana Campos viven cerca de Villatorres. Me pides su dirección. Aquí está: La granja de los Tres Robles, Carretera del Puente Nuevo cerca de Puerto Viejo. ¿Pero por qué Villatorres? No es un pueblo muy apasionante. De todas formas, tienen una habitación para ti y yo te los recomiendo. La casa es tranquila y la comida es buena. Bueno, buen viaje.

Isabel

Dear Ramón,

Thank you for your letter. Yes, Antonio and Ana Campos live close to Villatorres. You ask me for their address. Here it is: The Tres Robles farm, Carretera del Puente Nuevo, near Puerto Viejo. But why Villatores? It's not a very exciting village. Anyhow, they have a room for you and I recommend them to you. Their house is peaceful and the food is good. Well, have a good trip.

Isabel

Page 31   Picture puzzle

1c 2d 3b 4f 5e 6a

Page 33   Sancho Salchicha's disappearance

Villaloros

Sir,
Unfortunately, your father is probably dead. He knew our islands very well but at the time of his disappearance, he was looking for plants on some dangerous and very remote island. He was with two botanist friends. They had a good boat but it was the rainy season.

Pedro Peperoni, Governor of the islands

Page 35   Telling a story

Dos amigos, Miguel y Paco iban de compras, buscaban unos vaqueros. En una tienda, encontraron unas llaves en el bolsillo de unos vaqueros. Se las dieron al dueño de la tienda. "¡Las llaves de mi caja fuerte! ¡Gracias! Las perdí ayer. Las busqué por todas partes, pero no las encontré." Como recompensa, les dio los vaqueros.

Page 37   Say it in Spanish

*El señor Robón buscó la torre en ruinas, pero no la encontró.
Carmen, Fede y María fueron a la granja.
Encontraron al señor Robón.
Él no los vio.
Carmen y María se escondieron debajo de la ventana.
La mujer sirvió café.*

Page 39   The writing on the tower

We have kept this ruined tower because it is a sacred monument for the inhabitants of Villatorres.

The pirates of Pirates' Island destroyed it three years ago, but now, we have got our revenge. We have won our last battle against them, we have expelled them from their fort on the island and they have disappeared from our country.

Page 41   The false trail

Querido hijo: Ahora has encontrado todas las pistas que he dejado. Aquí está la última misión. Será difícil. Tendrás que ir a la comisaría de Puerto Viejo. Verás una ventana sin barrotes. Entrarás por allí. Dentro encontrarás una pared con paneles de madera. Todas mis joyas y mi fortuna están allí. Adiós S.S.

Dear son, Now you have found all the clues I left behind. Here is the last task. It will be difficult. You will have to go to the police station in Puerto Viejo. You will see a window without bars. You will get in through there. Inside you will find a wall with wooden panels. All my jewels and my fortune will be there. Farewell S.S.

Page 43   Talking about the future

*Su tren llegará a las tres.
Van a salir esta noche.
¿Qué vas a hacer?
Voy a ir a Villatorres mañana
Mañana sabremos cuándo (ella) va a venir.
Lo buscaremos.
Verá.
¿Vendrá (usted) conmigo?*

Page 45   ¿Cuál es el túnel más largo?

El túnel más largo es el túnel de María OR Es el túnel de María.

Page 47   What if?

*¡Lo gastaría todo!
Haría reparar el tejado.
Te compraría una bicicleta nueva.
Iríamos todos a ver a mi tía a Canadá.*

Page 48   María's letter

Monday, September 2nd

Dear Fede and Carmen,
Here's the article from The Villatorres Voice that tells our story. It's brilliant! What are you going to do with your share of the reward? I'm going to buy a radio-cassette player with mine.

If your Mum agrees, I'll come to your place during the Christmas holidays, so see you soon, I hope!

Love and kisses, María

The newspaper article

The Salchicha family treasure

María Salchicha with her friends Fede and Carmen and her dog, Guau Guau

Ramón Robón, the endangered bird thief who wanted to steal the family treasure

For María Salchicha and her friends Fede and Carmen, this has been an exciting month of August. They found a treasure and they helped the police to catch a crook.

A few months ago, Robón was on one of the Lorazul islands. He was looking for some endangered parrots there that he wanted to steal. He came across a letter from María's great-grandfather, Sancho. It was an old letter addressed to María's grandfather, Santiago, and left on the island in an old chest after Sancho's death. The letter was the first clue in a treasure hunt. It took Robón to Villatorres, where, stupidly, he lost it. Fede and Carmen, who were coming to spend a few days with their friend María, found it. The three teenagers managed to find the treasure (gold), hidden in the old Pirates' Fort, before the crook, and they helped the police to catch him.

The three heroes also received a reward of 300,000 pesetas from the police. Our congratulations to them!

Numbers and other useful words

Here you will find some useful lists of words and expressions. Remember that telling the time is explained on page 24 and directions are on page 15.

2,100 *dos mil cien*
100,000 *cien mil*
1,000,000 *un millón*

pasado mañana	the day after tomorrow
esta semana	this week
la semana pasada/que viene	last/next week

Essential expressions

buenos días	hello, good morning
buenas tardes	good afternoon, good evening
buenas noches	good evening, good night
adiós	goodbye
hola	hello, hi
hasta pronto	see you soon
hasta luego	see you later
sí	yes
no	no
tal vez	maybe
por favor	please
gracias	thank you
muchas gracias	thank you very much
de nada	you're welcome
perdón	excuse me
lo siento	I'm sorry
no entiendo	I don't understand
no sé	I don't know
¿Qué significa esta palabra?	What does this word mean?
¿Cómo se dice esto en español?	What's the Spanish for this?

(handwritten note: esta)
(handwritten note: esto)

Numbers

0	*cero*	17	*diecisiete*
1	*uno*	18	*dieciocho*
2	*dos*	19	*diecinueve*
3	*tres*	20	*veinte*
4	*cuatro*	21	*veintiuno*
5	*cinco*	22	*veintidós*
6	*seis*	23	*veintitrés*
7	*siete*	26	*veintiséis*
8	*ocho*	30	*treinta*
9	*nueve*	31	*treinta y uno*
10	*diez*	32	*treinta y dos*
11	*once*	40	*cuarenta*
12	*doce*	50	*cincuenta*
13	*trece*	60	*sesenta*
14	*catorce*	70	*setenta*
15	*quince*	80	*ochenta*
16	*dieciséis*	90	*noventa*

100	*cien*
101	*ciento uno*
150	*ciento cincuenta*
200	*doscientos*
300	*trescientos*
1,000	*mil*
1,100	*mil cien*
2,000	*dos mil*

"First", "second", "third", etc.

The Spanish for "first" is *primero* (*primera* in the feminine). *Primero* becomes *primer* before a masculine noun.

(el/la) segundo(a)	(the) second
(el/la) tercero(a)[1]	(the) third
(el/la) cuarto(a)	(the) fourth
(el/la) quinto(a)	(the) 5th
(el/la) sexto(a)	(the) 6th
(el/la) séptimo(a)	(the) 7th
(el/la) octavo(a)	(the) 8th
(el/la) noveno(a)	(the) 9th
(el/la) décimo(a)	(the) 10th

Months, seasons and days

enero	January
febrero	February
marzo	March
abril	April
mayo	May
junio	June
julio	July
agosto	August
septiembre	September
octubre	October
noviembre	November
diciembre	December
la primavera	spring
el verano	summer
el otoño	autumn, fall
el invierno	winter
lunes [m]	Monday
martes [m]	Tuesday
miércoles [m]	Wednesday
jueves [m]	Thursday
viernes [m]	Friday
sábado [m]	Saturday
domingo [m]	Sunday
el mes	month
la estación	season
el año	year
el día	day
la semana	week
el fin de semana	weekend
ayer	yesterday
hoy	today
mañana	tomorrow
antes de ayer, anteayer	the day before yesterday

Dates

la agenda	diary, notebook
el calendario	calendar
¿Qué día es hoy?	What's the date?
el lunes	on Monday
en agosto, en el mes de agosto	in August
el primero/el uno de abril	1st April
el dos de enero	2nd January
martes, 7 de septiembre	Tuesday, September 7th

1992	*mil novecientos noventa y dos*
1993	*mil novecientos noventa y tres*
1999	*mil novecientos noventa y nueve*
2000	*dos mil*

Weather

el tiempo	weather
el clima	climate
el pronóstico del tiempo	weather forecast
la temperatura	temperature
¿Qué temperatura hace?	What's the temperature?
¿Qué tiempo hace?	What's the weather like?
Hace bueno. Hace buen tiempo.	It's fine.
Hace malo. Hace mal tiempo.	The weather's bad.
Llueve. Está lloviendo.	It's raining.
Hace calor.	It's hot.
Hace sol.	It's sunny.
El sol brilla.	The sun's shining.
Hace frío.	It's cold.
Nieva. Está nevando.	It's snowing.
Hay hielo.	It's icy.
Hay niebla.	It's foggy.
el cielo	sky
el sol	sun
la lluvia	rain
la nube	cloud
el relámpago	lightning
el trueno	thunder
el hielo/la helada	frost
la nieve	snow
el granizo	hail

1 *Tercero* becomes *tercer* before a masculine noun.

Spanish-English word list

This list contains all the Spanish words from the illustrated section of this book, along with their pronunciations and English translations.

[m], [f] and [pl] are used as throughout the book (see Key, page 3).

Adjectives

Adjectives that have different forms in the masculine and feminine are listed in the masculine form with a bracketed "a" on the end. To get the feminine form, put the "a" on the end of the masculine form and drop the "o" if there is one.

Verbs

* shows a verb that is irregular in the present tense. Stem-changing verbs are shown with their stem change in brackets.

Pronunciation

The centre column shows you how to pronounce each word. The way to say the words properly is to imitate Spanish speakers and apply the rules given on pages 4–5. However, by reading the "words" in this column as if they were English, you will get a good idea of how to say things, or you will remember the sound of words you have heard before.

Note that, in this pronunciation column, the Spanish **j** is shown as "ch". Remember, it is a slightly rasping sound similar to the "ch" in the Scottish word "loch", or a bit like the "h" in "hate". Also note that in this column, capital letters show which part of the word you should stress.

A

a	a	to, at (for time)
a la derecha	a la derETsha	(to/on the) right
a la izquierda	a la eethKYERda	(to/on the) left
a la sombra	a la ssOMbra	in the shade
a menudo	ameNOOdo	often
¿a qué hora?	akeOra	(at) what time?
a veces	aBEthess	sometimes
abandonado(a)	abandoNAdo	abandoned, left
abrazos	aBRAthoss	hugs, love from (at end of letter)
abrir	aBREER	to open
la abuela	la aBWEla	grandmother
el abuelo	el aBWElo	grandfather
acercarse	atherKARsse	to come next to (me/you...)
acostarse (ue)	akossTARsse	to go to bed
adiós	adeeOSS	goodbye, farewell
el/la adolescente	el/la adolessTHENte	teenager [m/f]
adorar	adoRAR	to worship
el aeropuerto	el aeroPWERto	airport
afeitarse	afeyTARsse	to shave
afortunadamente	afortoonadaMENte	luckily, fortunately, happily
la agenda	la aCHENda	diary, notebook
la agente de policía	la aCHENte de poleeTHEEya	policewoman
ahí	aEE	there
ahora	aOra	now
ahora mismo	aOraMEEZmo	straight/right away
al final de	alfeeNAL de	at/to the end of
al lado de	al LAdo de	by, next to
algo	ALgo	something
algún/alguno(a)	alGOON/alGOOno	some
algunos(as)	alGOOnoss	a few, some
allí, allá	alYEE, alYA	(over) there
alquilar	alkeeLAR	to hire, to rent
alto	ALto	stop
alto(a)	ALto	tall, high
amable	aMAble	kind, nice
amarillo(a)	amaREELyo	yellow
la amiga	la aMEEga	friend [f]
el amigo	el aMEEgo	friend [m]
andar	anDAR	to walk
la anilla	la aNEELya	ring (on a wall)
el anillo	el aNEELyo	ring (on finger)
el año	el ANyo	year
anoche	aNOTshe	yesterday evening, last night
ante	ANte	before, in front of
antes	ANtess	before
antes de ayer, anteayer	ANtess de aYER, anteaYER	the day before yesterday
antes que	ANtesske	before
antiguo(a)	anTEEgwo	old, antique
apasionante	apassyoNANte	exciting
aquel [m], aquella [f], aquellos [m pl], aquellas [f pl]	aKELL, aKELLya, aKELLyoss, aKELLyass	that, those

aquél [m], aquélla [f], aquéllos [m pl], aquéllas [f pl]	aKELL, AKELLya, aKELLyoss, aKELLyass	that (one over there), those (ones over there)
aquello	aKELLyo	that one
aquí	aKEE	here
el árbol	el ARbol	tree
arreglar	arrreGLAR	to repair, to mend
el artículo	el arTEEkoolo	article
así	aSSEE	so, thus, in this way, like that
así que	aSSEEke	then, so
la aspirina	la asspeeREEna	aspirin
asqueroso(a)	asskeROsso	dirty, horrible, revolting
atrapar	atraPAR	to catch
aún	aOOn	yet, still
ayer	aYER	yesterday
ayer por la noche	aYER por la NOTshe	yesterday evening, last night
ayer por la tarde	aYER por la TARde	yesterday evening/afternoon
ayudar a	ayooDAR a	to help
azul	aTHOOL	blue

B

bajar	baCHAR	to go down
el banco	el BANGko	bench, bank
la barca	la BARka	(rowing) boat
el barco	el BARko	ship, boat
la barrera	la baRRRERa	gate, barrier
el barrote	el baRRROte	bar (on window)
bastante	bassTANte	quite
la batalla	la baTALya	battle
(muchos) besos	(MOOTshoss) BEssos	(lots of) kisses
la bici	la BEEthee	bike
la bicicleta	la beetheeKLEta	bicycle
bien	bYEN	good, right, OK, well
la bisabuela	el beessaBWEla	great-grandmother
el bisabuelo	la beessaBWElo	great-grandfather
blanco(a)	bLANGko	white
el bolsillo	el bolSSEELyo	pocket
el bolso	el BOLsso	bag
bonito(a)	boNEEto	pretty
el bosque	el BOSSke	forest, wood
el botánico	el boTAneeko	botanist
brillar	breeLYAR	to shine
la broma	la BROma	joke
buen viaje	bWEN beeAche	have a good trip
buenas noches	bwenass NOTshess	good evening/night
buenas tardes	bwenass TARdess	good afternoon, hello (p.m.)
bueno	BWEno	well, right, all right, good
bueno(a)	BWEno	good
buenos días	bwenoss DEEyas	good morning, hello (a.m.)
buscar	boossKAR	to look for
la búsqueda del tesoro	la BOOSkeda del teSSOro	treasure hunt

C

la cabra	la KAbra	goat
caer en la trampa	kaER enlaTRAMpa	to fall in the trap, to fall for it
caerse	kaERsse	to fall
el café	el kaFE	café, coffee
la caja	la KAcha	box
la caja fuerte	la kachaFWERte	safe, strong-box
el calabozo	el kalaBOtho	dungeon
cállate	KALyate	quiet, be quiet
la calle	la KALye	street
calmarse	kalMARsse	to calm down
calvo(a)	KALbo	bald
la cámara de fotos	la KAmara de FOtoss	camera
el camino	el kaMEEno	path, way
la camisa	la kaMEEssa	shirt
la camiseta	la kameeSSEta	T-shirt, vest
el camping	el KAMpeen	campsite
el campo	el KAMpo	field, countryside
Canadá	kanaDA	Canada
el cangrejo	el kanGREcho	crab
cansado(a)	kanSSAdo	tired
cantar	kanTAR	to sing
capturar	kaptooRAR	to catch
el caramelo	el karaMElo	sweet, candy
caro(a)	KAro	expensive
la carretera (principal)	la karrreTEra (preentheePAL)	(main) road
la carta	la KARta	letter, menu
las cartas	lass KARtass	(playing) cards
la casa	la KAssa	house, home
casi	KAssee	almost, nearly
el castillo	el kassTEELyo	castle
los catalejos	loss kataLEchoss	binoculars
la cena	la THEna	supper, evening meal
cenar	theNAR	to have supper
cerca de	THERka de	close to, near
cerrado(a)	theRRRAdo	closed, shut
cerrado(a) con llave	theRRRAdo kon LYAbe	locked
la cerradura	la therrraDOOra	lock
cerrar (ie)	theRRRAR	to close, to shut
la cesta	la THESSta	basket
el chandal	el tshanDAL	track suit
la chaqueta	la tshaKEta	jacket
la chica	la TSHEEka	girl
el chico	el TSHEEko	boy
el cielo	el THYElo	sky
el cine	el THEEne	cinema
la cinta	la THEENta	ribbon, tape
la ciudad	la THYOOdath	town
claro	KLAro	of course
la coca-cola	la kokaKOla	coca-cola, cola
el cofre	el KOfre	chest
coger	koGER	to pick up, to take
la colección	la kolekTHYON	collection
el colegio	el koLEcheeyo	school
la colina	la koLEEna	hill
comer	koMER	to eat
la comida	la koMEEda	food, lunch
la comisaría	la komeessaREEa	police station
como	KOmo	as
cómo	KOmo	how
¿cómo?	KOmo	how?
la compañera	la kompanYEra	mate, good friend [f]
el compañero	el kompanYEro	mate, good friend [m]
comprar	komPRAR	to buy
con	KON	with
con cariño	kon kaREENyo	with love
conducir*	kondooTHEER	to drive
conmigo	konMEEgo	with me
conocer*	konoTHER	to know
conservar	konsserBAR	to keep, to preserve
el constructor	el konsstrookTOR	builder
construir*	konsstrooEER	to build
contar (ue)	konTAR	to tell, to count
contento(a)	konTENto	pleased, happy
contigo	konTEEgo	with you
continuar	konteenooAR	to follow, to go/carry on
contra	KONtra	against
correos	koRRREoss	post office
cortar	korTAR	to cut

corto(a)	KORto	short
la costa	la KOSSta	coast
costar (ue)	kossTAR	to cost
cruzar	krooTHAR	to cross
el cuadro	el KWAdro	painting, picture
¿cuál?	KWAL	which (one)?
cualquier cosa	kwalkeeyer KOssa	anything
¿cuándo?	KWANdo	when?
¿cuánto(a)?	KWANto	how much?
¿cuántos(as)?	KWANtoss	how many?
cuarto(a)	KWARto	fourth
la cuerda	la KWERda	rope
la cueva	la KWEba	cave
cuidado	kooeeDAdo	watch out, careful

D

el dado	el DAdo	die (pl: dice)
dar*	DAR	to give
dar* las gracias	dar lass GRAtheeyass	to thank
de	de	of, from, by
¿de dónde?	de DONde	where... from?, from where?
de prisa	de PREEssa	quick, quickly
¿de quién?	de keeYENN	whose?
de todas formas	de todass FORmass	anyhow
de verdad	de berDAth	real, true
de vez en cuando	deBETH enKWANdo	sometimes
debajo de	deBAcho de	under, underneath
deber	deBER	to have to, must
decir	deTHEER	to say
dejar	deCHAR	to leave (behind)
delante de	deLANte de	in front of
demasiado	demaSSYAdo	too
dentro (de)	DENtro (de)	inside
desaparecer*	dessapareTHER	to disappear
la desaparición	la dessapareeTHYON	disappearance
descifrar	desstheeFRAR	to decipher, to figure out
desde	DEZde	from, since
desierto(a)	deSSYERto	deserted, desert
despacio	dessPATHyo	slowly
despertarse (ie)	dessperTARsse	to wake up
después	dessPWESS	later, then
destruir	desstrooEEr	to destroy
el desván	el dezBAN	attic
el detalle	el deTALLye	detail
detenido(a)	deteNEEdo	under arrest
detrás de	deTRASS de	behind
devolver (ue)	debolBER	to bring/take back
el día	el DEEa	day
dibujar	deebooCHAR	to draw
el dibujo	el deeBOOcho	drawing
difícil	deeFEEtheel	difficult, hard
el dinero	el deeNEro	money
la dirección	la deerekTHYON	address, direction
dirigido(a) a	deereeCHEEdo a	addressed to
¿dónde?	DONde	where?
dormir (ue)	dorMEER	to sleep
dos	doss	two
el dueño	el DWENyo	owner, landlord
durante	dooRANte	during

E

el edificio	el edeeFEETHyo	building
él	el	he
ella	ELya	she
ellos(as)	ELyoss	they
empezar (ie)	empeTHAR	to begin, to start
en	en	in, at, on
en alguna parte	en alGOOna PARte	somewhere
en el momento de	en el moMENto de	at the time of
en ninguna parte	en neenGOOna PARte	nowhere
en primer lugar	en preeMER looGAR	first of all
en ruinas	en rrrooEEnass	ruined, in ruins
en todas partes	en TOdass PARtess	everywhere
encima de	enTHEEma de	on, over
encontrar (ue)	enkonTRAR	to find, to meet

encontrarse (ue)	enkonTRARsse	to be (found/situated), to find by chance, to come across
enfermo(a)	enFERmo	ill, unwell
enfrente de	enFRENte de	opposite
la ensalada	la enssaLAda	salad
enseñar	ensseNYAR	to show, to teach
ensuciar	enssooTHYAR	to dirty
entender (ie)	entenDER	to understand
entonces	enTONthess	then, so
la entrada	la enTRAda	entrance
entrar	enTRAR	to go in, to enter
entre	ENtre	between, among
enviar por fax	emBYAR por FASS	to fax, to send a fax
envolver (ue)	embolBER	to wrap up
equivocado(a)	ekeeboKAdo	wrong
es	ess	(it) is
el escalón	el eskaLON	step
esconder	eskonDER	to hide (a thing or person)
esconderse	eskonDERsse	to hide (yourself)
ese [m], esa [f], esos [m pl], esas [f pl]	Esse, Essa, Essoss, Essass	that, those
ése [m], ésa [f], ésos [m pl], ésas [f pl]	Esse, Essa, Essoss, Essass	that (one), those (ones)
eso	esso	that (one)
España	essPANya	Spain
el esparadrapo	el essparaDRApo	plaster(s), (adhesive bandage)
esperar (a)	esspeRAR (a)	to wait (for), to hope, to expect
está	essTA	(it) is
está bien	essTA BYEN	(it's) all right
esta mañana	ESSta manYAna	this morning
la estación	la esstaTHYON	station, season
el estafador	el esstafaDOR	crook, swindler
están	essTAN	(they) are
estar*	essTAR	to be
estar* de acuerdo	essTAR de aKWERdo	to agree
este [m], esta [f], estos [m pl], estas [f pl]	ESSte, ESSta, ESStoss, ESStass	this, these
éste [m], ésta [f], éstos [m pl], éstas [f pl]	ESSte, ESSta, ESStoss, ESStass	this (one), these (ones)
esto	ESSto	this (one)
el/la estudiante	el, la esstooDYANte	student [m/f]
estudiar	esstooDYAR	to study
el estudio	el essTOOdeeyo	studio, study
estúpidamente	essTOOpeedamente	stupidly
Europa	eooROpa	Europe
exactamente	essaktaMENte	exactly
examinar	essameeNAR	to examine
la excursión	la esskoorSSYON	outing, trip
explicar	esspleeKAR	to explain
explorar	essploRAR	to explore
expulsar	esspoolSSAR	to expel
en extinción, en peligro de extinción	en essteenTHYON, en peLEEgro de essteenTHYON	endangered

F

fácil	FAtheel	easy
la falda	la FALda	skirt
falso(a)	FALsso	false
faltar	falTAR	to be missing
la familia	la faMEELya	family
la farmacia	la farMAtheeya	chemist's, pharmacy
felicitar	feleetheeTAR	to congratulate
felizmente	feleethMENte	luckily, fortunately, happily
fenomenal	fenomeNAL	brilliant
feo(a)	FEo	ugly
el filete	el fiLEte	steak
la fortuna	la forTOOna	fortune
la foto	la FOto	photo
la fotocopiadora	la fotokopeeaDOra	photocopier
la fresa	la FREssa	strawberry
frío(a)	FREEo	cold
la fuente	la FWENte	fountain
fuera	FWERa	outside
fuera de	FWERA de	outside
fuerte	FWERte	loud(ly), strong(ly)

el fuerte	el FWERte	fort
funcionar	foonthyoNAR	to work, to function

G

las gafas	lass GAfass	glasses
ganar	gaNAR	to win, to earn
gastar	gassTAR	to spend (money)
el gato	el GAto	cat
girar	cheeRAR	to turn
el gobernador	el gobernaDOR	governor
la gorra	la GOrrra	cap
gracias	GRAtheeyass	thank you, thanks
grande	GRANde	big, old
la granja	la GRANcha	farm
gris	greess	grey
la guerra	la GErrra	war
la guía	la GEEa	guidebook
la guitarra	la GEEtarrra	guitar
gustar	goossTAR	to please

H

había	aBEEa	there was/were
la habitación	la abeetaTHYON	room, bedroom
el habitante	el abeeTANte	inhabitant
habitualmente	abeetooalMENte	usually, normally
hablar	aBLAR	to talk, to speak
habrá	aBRA	there will be
hace	Athe	ago
hacer*	aTHER	to do, to make
hacer* círculos	aTHER SSEErkooloss	to go round and round, to go around in circles
hacer* compras	aTHER KOMprass	to do some shopping
hacer* una pregunta	aTHER oona preGOONta	to ask a question
hacia	Atheeya	toward, about
la hamburguesa	la amboorGEssa	hamburger
hasta	ASSta	until
hasta luego	assta LWEgo	see you later
hasta pronto	assta PRONto	see you soon
hay	Aee	there is/are
hay que	Aeeke	you must, one has to
el helado	el eLAdo	ice cream
la hermana	la erMAna	sister
el hermano	el erMAno	brother
el héroe	el Erowe	hero
las herramientas	lass erraMYENtass	tools
el hierro	el YErrro	iron
la hija	la EEcha	daughter
el hijo	el EEcho	son
la historia	la eessTOreeya	story, history
la hoja	la Ocha	leaf, sheet (of paper)
hola	Ola	hello
el hombre	el OMbre	man
el hotel	el oTEL	hotel
hoy	Oy	today
el huésped	el WESSpeth	lodger, boarder

I

la idea	la eeDEa	idea
la iglesia	la eeGLEsseeya	church
igual	eeGWAL	(the same
interesante	eentereSSANte	interesting
la intersección	la eentersekTHYON	junction
ir*	eer	to go
ir* de compras	eer de KOMprass	to go shopping
irse*	EERsse	to go, to go away, to be off
la isla	la EESSla	island

J

el jardín	el charDEEN	garden
el jersey	el cherSSEY	sweater
joven	CHOben	young
la joya	la CHOya	jewel
jugar (ue)	chooGAR	to play
junto a	CHOONto a	next to

K

el kilo (de)	*el KEElo (de)*	kilo (of)

L

ladrar	*laDRAR*	to bark
el ladrón	*el laDRON*	burglar, thief
el lago	*el LAgo*	lake
lanzar	*lanTHAR*	to throw
el lápiz (de colores),	*el LApeeth, loss*	crayon
los lápices [pl]	*LApeethess*	
largo(a)	*LARgo*	long
lavarse	*laBARsse*	to wash (yourself)
leer	*LEer*	to read
lejos de	*LEchoss de*	far from
lento	*LENto*	slowly
levantarse	*lebanTARsse*	to get up
el libro	*el LEEbro*	book
la lima	*la LEEma*	nail file
la linterna	*la leenTERna*	torch, flashlight
se llama	*sseLYAma*	his/her/its name is
llamarse	*lyaMARsse*	to be called
la llave	*la LYAbe*	key
llegar	*lyeGAR*	to arrive, to reach, to get
llevar	*lyeBAR*	to carry, to wear, to take
llover (ue)	*lyoBER*	to rain
lo siento	*lo SSYENto*	I'm sorry
lograr	*loGRAR*	to manage
el loro	*el LOro*	parrot
la lupa	*la LOOpa*	magnifying glass
la luz	*la LOOTH*	light

M

la madera	*la maDEra*	wood
la madre	*la MAdre*	mother
la madrugada	*la madrooGAda*	morning (midnight to 5 or 6 a.m.), the small hours
el maestro	*el maESStro*	teacher
el mago	*el MAgo*	magician
mal	*mal*	bad, badly
la maleta	*la maLEta*	suitcase
el maletín	*el maleTEEN*	briefcase
malo(a)	*MAlo*	bad
mamá	*maMA*	Mum, Mom
mañana	*manYAna*	tomorrow
la mañana	*la manYAna*	morning
mañana por la mañana	*manYAna porla manYAna*	tomorrow morning
la mandarina	*la mandaREEna*	mandarin
la manzana	*la manTHAna*	apple
el mapa	*el MApa*	map
la máquina	*la MAkeena*	machine
el mar	*el MAR*	sea
marrón	*maRRRON*	brown
más	*mass*	more
el/la/los/las más	*el/la/loss/lass MASS*	the most
mayor	*maYOR*	bigger, older
el/la/los/las mayor(es)	*el/la/loss/lass maYOr(ess)*	the biggest, the oldest
me llamo	*me LYAmo*	my name is (I am called)
la medianoche	*la medeeaNOTshe*	midnight
el mediodía	*el medeeoDEEya*	midday
mejor	*meCHOR*	better
el/la/los/las mejor(es)	*el/la/loss/lass meCHOr(ess)*	the best
menor	*meNOR*	smaller, younger
el/la/los/las menor(es)	*el/la/loss/lass meNOr(ess)*	the smallest, the youngest
menos	*meNOSS*	fewer, less
el mercado	*el merKAdo*	market
el mes	*el MESS*	month
la mesa	*la MEssa*	table
meter	*meTER*	to put in/inside
el metro	*ellMEtro*	underground (railway)
mirar	*meeRAR*	to look (at)
la misión	*la meeSSYON*	task

el mismo [m]**, la misma** [f]**, los mismos** [m pl]**, las mismas** [f pl]	*el MEEZmo, la MEEZma, loss MEEZmoss, las MEEZmass*	the (very) same
la mochila	*la motSHEEla*	backpack
mojado(a)	*moCHAdo*	wet
molestar	*molessTAR*	to disturb
un momento	*un moMENto*	one moment, just a minute
la montaña	*la monTANya*	mountain
el monumento	*el monooMENto*	monument
morir (ue)	*moREER*	to die
mover	*moBER*	to move
mucho	*MOOTsho*	a lot, lots, really
mucho(a)	*MOOTsho*	a lot of, lots of, many
el muelle	*el MWELye*	quay, dock
la muerte	*la MWERte*	death
muerto(a)	*MWERto*	dead
la mujer	*la mooCHER*	woman
muy	*MOOy*	very, really, most

N

nada	*NAda*	nothing
nadar	*naDAR*	to swim
nadie	*NAdeeye*	nobody
la naranja	*la naRANcha*	orange
Navidad	*nabeeDATH*	Christmas
necesitar	*nethesseeTAR*	to need
negro(a)	*NEgro*	black
ningún(a)	*neenGOON*	none, no
el niño	*el NEENyo*	child, boy
no	*no*	no, not
no...aún	*no...aOON*	not...yet
no importa	*no eemPORta*	it doesn't matter
no lo sé	*noloSSE*	I don't know [it]
no...nada	*no...NAda*	not...anything
no...nadie	*no...NAdeeye*	not...anybody
no...ningún(a)	*no...neenGOON*	not any (at all)
no...nunca	*no...NOONka*	not...ever
no...todavía	*no...todaBEEya*	not...yet
no...ya	*no...ya*	not...any more
la noche	*la NOTshe*	evening, night
nosotros(as)	*noSSOtross*	we
la nota	*la NOta*	note
Nueva York	*NWEba YOR*	New York
nuevo(a)	*NWEbo*	new
el número	*el NOOmero*	number
nunca	*NOONka*	never

O

o	*o*	or
ocultar	*okoolTAR*	to hide
la oficina de correos, correos	*la ofeeTHEEna de koRRREoss, koRRREoss*	post office
oler (hue)	*oLER*	to smell
olvidarse	*olbeeDARsse*	to forget
ordenar	*ordeNAR*	to tidy up
la oreja	*la OREcha*	ear
el oro	*el Oro*	gold
otro(a)	*Otro*	other, another (one)

P

el padre	*el PAdre*	father
los padres	*loss PAdress*	parents
pagar	*paGAR*	to pay
el país	*el paEESS*	country
el paisaje	*el paeeSSAche*	landscape
el pájaro	*el PAcharo*	bird
el pan	*el PAN*	bread
el panel	*el paNEL*	panel
el pantalón	*el pantaLON*	trousers
los pantalones cortos	*loss pantaLOness korTOSS*	shorts
papá	*paPA*	Dad, Daddy
el papel	*el paPEL*	paper
el par	*el PAR*	pair

Spanish	Pronunciation	English
para	PAra	for, toward, to, in order to, so as to
parecer*	pareTHER	to look, to seem, to appear
la pared	la paRETH	wall (indoors)
la pareja	la paREcha	couple, pair
el parque	el PARke	park
la parte	la PARte	part, share
pasado(a)	paSSAdo	last, past
pasado mañana	paSSAdo manYAna	the day after tomorrow
pasar	paSSAR	to pass, to hand, to spend (time)
pasarlo (muy) bien	paSSARlo (mooy) BYEN	to have (lots of) fun
el paso de peatones	el PAsso de peaTOness	pedestrian crossing
el pastel	el passTEL	cake
las patatas fritas	lass paTAtass FREEtass	chips, French fries
el pedazo	el peDAtho	piece, bit
pedir (i)	peDEER	to order, to ask for
peligroso(a)	peleeGROsso	dangerous
pensar (ie)	penSSAR	to think
peor	peOR	worse
el/la/los/las peor(es)	el/la/loss/lass peOR	the worst
pequeño(a)	peKENyo	small, little
perder (ie)	perDER	to lose, to miss
perdón	perDON	sorry, excuse me
perfecto(a)	perFEKto	perfect
el periódico	el pereeOdeeko	newspaper
pero	PEro	but
el perro	PErro	dog
la peseta	la peSSEta	peseta (Spanish money)
la piedra	la PYEdra	stone
el pirata	el peeRAta	pirate
la piscina	la peessTHEEna	swimming pool
la pista	la PEESSta	clue
la planta	la PLANta	plant
la playa	la PLAya	beach
la plaza	la PLAtha	square
poco	POko	few, little
poder (ue)	poDER	to be allowed to, can, may, might
el policía	el poleeTHEEya	policeman
la policía	la poleeTHEEya	the police
poner*	poNER	to put
por	por	for (because of), through, along
por allí	por alYEE	that way, over/around there
por aquí	por aKEE	over/around here, this way
por desgracia	por dezGRAtheeya	unfortunately, sadly
por favor	por faBOR	please
por fin	por FEEN	at last
por fortuna	por forTOOna	luckily
¿por qué?	por KE	why?
por todas partes	por todass PARtess	everywhere
porque	porKE	because
la postal	la possTAL	postcard
precioso(a)	pretheeOsso	lovely, beautiful
preferir (ie)	prefeREER	to prefer
la pregunta	la preGOONta	question
preocuparse	preokooPARsse	to worry
preparado(a)	prepaRAdo	ready, prepared
prestar	pressTAR	to lend
primer/primero(a)	preeMER	first
primero	preeMEro	first (of all)
probablemente	probableMENte	probably
probar (ue)	proBAR	to taste, to try
prohibido(a)	proeeBEEdo	forbidden
pronto	PRONto	soon, early
próximo(a)	PROKsseemo	next
el pueblo	el PWEblo	village
el puente	el PWENte	bridge
la puerta	la PWERta	door
el puerto	el PWERto	port

Q

que	ke	who(m), which, than
¡qué!	ke	how!, what!
¿qué?	ke	what?, which?
¡qué bien!	ke BYEN	great!
¿qué es eso?	ke ess Esso	what is that?
¿qué hora es?	keOra ess	what time is it?, what's the time?
!qué le vamos a hacer!	ke le BAmoss a aTHER	too bad!
querer (ie)	keRER	to want, to love
querido(a)	keREEdo	dear
querría	keRRREEya	I would like
el queso	el kEsso	cheese
quien, quienes [pl]	keeEN, keeENess	who(m), which
¿quién?, ¿quiénes? [pl]	keeEN, keeENess	who?
quisiera	keesseeYEra	I would like
quizá	keeTHA	maybe, perhaps

R

el radiocassette	e rrradeeokaSSEte	radio-cassette player
rápidamente	RRRApeedamente	quickly
rápido(a)	RRRApeedo	quick, quickly
raro(a)	RRRaro	weird, strange, odd, unusual
el rastro	el RRRASStro	trail
realmente	rrealMENte	really
recibir	rrretheeBEER	to receive, to get
recomendar (ie)	rrrekomenDAR	to recommend
la recompensa	la rrrekomPENssa	reward
reconocer*	rrrekonoTHER	to recognize
recordar (ue)	rrrekorDAR	to remember
la red	la RRRETH	net
regalar	rrregaLAR	to treat (someone to), to give, to offer
regresar	rrregreSSAR	to come/go (back)
remar	rrreMAR	to row
el remo	el RRREmo	oar
remoto(a)	rrreMOto	remote, far away
la remuneración	la rrremooneraTHYON	fee, payment
reparar	rrrepaRAR	to have mended, to fix
repetir (i)	rrrepeTEER	to repeat
la respuesta	la rrressPWEssta	answer
el restaurante	el rrresstaooRANte	restaurant
el retrato	el rrreTRAto	portrait
la reunión	la rrreooNYON	meeting
rico(a)	RRREEko	rich
el río	el RRREEyo	river
robar	rrroBAR	to steal, to rob
el robo	el RRRObo	theft
la roca	la RRROka	rock
rocoso(a)	rrroKOsso	rocky
rojo(a)	RRROcho	red
romper	rrromPER	to break (something)
romperse	rrromPERsse	to break
roñoso(a)	rrroNYOsso	rusty, filthy
la ropa	la RRROpa	clothes, clothing
roto(a)	RRROto	broken
la ruina	la rrrooEEna	ruin

S

Spanish	Pronunciation	English
saber*	ssaBER	to know
el sabor	el ssaBOR	flavour, taste
sacar fotos	ssaKAR FOtoss	to take photos
sagrado(a)	ssaGRAdo	sacred
la salida	la ssaLEEda	exit
salir*	ssaLEER	to go out, to leave
se busca	sseBOOSSka	wanted
se puede	ssePWEde	it is possible to, one you can
el secreto	el sseKREto	secret
seguir (i)	sseGEER	to follow, to carry on, to continue
según	sseGOON	according to
segundo(a)	sseGOONdo	second
seguramente	ssegooraMENte	probably
seguro que	sseGOOro ke	definitely, most probably
el semáforo	el sseMAforo	traffic lights
la señal	la sseNYAL	sign
(el) señor (Sr.)	(el) ssenYOR	Mr
(la) señora (Sra.)	(la) ssenYORa	Mrs
(la) señorita	(la) ssenyoREEta	Miss

Spanish	Pronunciation	English
sentirse (ie) bien/mal	ssenTEERsse BYEN/MAL	to feel well/not well
ser*	sser	to be
ser* de noche	sser de NOTshe	to be night-time/dark
servir (i)	sserBEER	to serve
si	ssee	if
sí	ssee	yes
siempre	SYEMpre	always
silencio	sseeLENtheeyo	quiet, be quiet
simpático(a)	sseemPAteeko	nice
sin	sseen	without
el sitio	el SSEEteeyo	place
sobre	SSObre	above, over, on top of
el sol	el SSOL	sun
solamente	ssolaMENte	only
soler (ue)	ssoLER	to be used to, to be in the habit of, to usually/ normally . . .
solo(a)	SSOlo	alone
el sombrero	el ssomBREro	hat
el sombrero de copa	el ssomBREro de KOpa	top hat
son	sson	(they) are
son las . . .	sson lass	it is... (time)
la sopa	la SSOpa	soup
suficiente	ssoofeeTHYENte	enough
el supermercado	el ssoopermerKAdo	supermarket

T

Spanish	Pronunciation	English
tal vez	tal BETH	maybe, perhaps
también	tamBYEN	too, also, as well
tan	tan	so
tan . . . como	tan KOmo	(just) as...as
tarde	TARde	late
la tarde	la TARde	afternoon, evening
el té	el TE	(cup of) tea
el técnico	el TEKneeko	mechanic, technician
el tejado	el teCHAdo	roof
el templo	el TEMplo	temple
la temporada de lluvias	la tempoRAda de LYOObeeyass	rainy season
tener*	teNER	to have
el tenis	el TEneess	tennis
tercero(a)	terTHEro	third
terminarse	termeeNARsse	to end, to finish
el ternero	el terNEro	calf
el tesoro	el teSSOro	treasure
la tía	la TEEa	aunt
la tienda	la TYENda	shop
la tienda (de campaña)	la TYENda (de kamPANya)	tent
la tierra	la TYErrra	earth, soil, ground
tirar	teeRAR	to pull, to throw
tirar de	teeRAR de	to pull on, to give (something) a pull
la toalla	la toALya	towel
todavía	todaBEEa	still
todavía no	todaBEEa no	not yet
todo	TOdo	everything
todo(a)	TOdo	all, every
todo el mundo	todo el MOONdo	everyone, everybody
todo recto	TOdo RRREKto	straight ahead
tomar	toMAR	to take
tomar prestado	toMAR pressTAdo	to borrow
tonto(a)	TONto	stupid, daft
la torre	la TOrrre	tower
trabajar	trabaCHAR	to work
traer	traER	to bring
el traje	el TRAche	suit

Spanish	Pronunciation	English
la trampa	la TRAMpa	trap
tranquilo(a)	tranKEElo	quiet, peaceful, calm
tras	trass	after
la travesía	la trabeSSEEa	crossing
el tren	el TREN	train
tres	tress	three
el trozo	el TROtho	piece, bit
tú	too	you
el túnel	el TOOnel	tunnel
turístico(a)	tooREESSteeko	tourist(ic)

U

Spanish	Pronunciation	English
último(a)	OOLteemo	last
uno(a)	OOno, OOna	one
una cosa	OOna KOssa	something
unos(as)	OOnoss	some
usted (Ud.)	oossTETH	you
ustedes (Uds.)	oossTEdess	you

V

Spanish	Pronunciation	English
la vaca	la BAka	cow
las vacaciones	lass bakaTHYOness	holidays, vacations
vacío(a)	baTHEEyo	empty
valer	baLER	to cost
la valla	la BALya	fence
los vaqueros	loss baKEross	jeans
la vecina	la beTHEEna	neighbour [f]
el vecino	el beTHEEno	neighbour [m]
la vela	la BEla	candle
venga	BENga	come on, go on
vengarse	benGARsse	to get your revenge
venir*	beNEER	to come
la ventana	la benTAna	window
ver*	ber	to see
verdad	berDATH	true, right
verde	BERde	green
vestirse (i)	bessTEERsse	to dress, to get dressed
el veterinario	el betereeNAreeyo	vet
viejo(a)	BYEcho	old
visitar	beesseeTAR	to visit
vivir	beeBEER	to live
volver (ue)	bolBER	to return, to come/get back
vosotros(as)	boSSOtross	you
la voz	la BOTH	voice

Y

Spanish	Pronunciation	English
y	ee	and
ya	ya	any more, already, yet, now
ya basta	ya BASSta	it's/that's enough
ya (lo) sé	ya (lo) SSE	I know [it]
yo	yo	I, me

Z

Spanish	Pronunciation	English
las zapatillas (de deporte)	lass thapaTEELyass (de dePORte)	trainers
los zapatos	loss thaPAtoss	shoes
el zumo de manzana	el THOOmo de manTHAna	apple juice
el zumo de naranja	el THOOmo de naRANcha	orange juice

First published in 1992 by Usborne Publishing Ltd.
Usborne House, 83–85 Saffron Hill, London EC1N 8RT, England
Copyright © 1992 Usborne Publishing Ltd.

Printed in Great Britain.